Claire stepped forward with a look in her ~~eye~~ that would have made Jake take a step back if he hadn't already been pressed against the railing.

"Hi, Jake. Hi, Zoey. Is this a closed meeting of the mutual support society?"

"I was just asking Zoey if . . . if she was okay," Jake said.

"And is she?" Claire asked. The words were silky but cracked like a whip.

Jake nodded.

"Good," Claire said. "And have you checked with Louise Kronenberger lately to see if she's okay too?"

Jake flushed. He wasn't easily intimidated, but Claire was capable of an ice-cold fury that was just scary. In a part of his mind he couldn't help but admire her. "Not lately," he said.

"Too bad, because I like to make sure absolutely everyone is okay—Zoey, Louise, Lucas." She turned on Zoey. "Is Lucas okay, too?"

Zoey was blushing darkly, her face set in resentment. "Yes, he's okay," she said through gritted teeth.

"Just okay?" Claire demanded. "I'm a little surprised. I found him much, much better than just okay."

Get all the hot news from Chatham Island at
www.avonbooks.com/chathamisland

MAKING OUT #7

Lucas gets hurt

KATHERINE APPLEGATE

Originally published as *Boyfriends Girlfriends*

AN AVON FLARE BOOK

Grateful acknowledgment is made for the use of lyrics from *Sometimes I Slip* by Clarence "Gatemouth" Brown, copyright © Real Records, Inc.

Originally published by HarperPaperbacks as *Boyfriends Girlfriends*

AVON BOOKS, INC.
1350 Avenue of the Americas
New York, New York 10019

Copyright © 1994 by Daniel Weiss Associates, Inc., and
Katherine Applegate
Published by arrangement with Daniel Weiss Associates, Inc.
Library of Congress Catalog Card Number: 98-92793
ISBN: 0-380-80217-1
www.avonbooks.com/chathamisland

First Avon Flare Printing: December 1998

AVON FLARE TRADEMARK REG. U.S. PAT. OFF. AND IN OTHER COUNTRIES, MARCA REGISTRADA, HECHO EN U.S.A.

Printed in the U.S.A.

WCD 10 9 8 7 6 5 4 3

For Michael

"Sometimes things change so much you feel like you've come full circle and back to a place you've been before," Lucas said.

So. That's what this was about. Claire was a little surprised. Even a little disappointed in Lucas. "Full circle back to a beach a long time ago?" Claire asked, knowing the answer.

He nodded. "Our first kiss."

She should put an end to this. She really should. But the memories were strong for her, too. There had been a time when she would have done anything for Lucas Cabral. And it would be a down payment on paying Jake back. "Are you going to ask me as politely as you did then, Lucas, with your voice all squeaky and trembling?" she said, half-mocking, half-trembling with anticipation.

Lucas slid across the car seat toward her, closer, close enough that the slightest movement would bring them together. "Do I have to ask?"

"No," Claire said. "You don't."

"Look man, look man, no, look, don't man. Don't shoot me, man."

He was begging. Praying to Christopher like he

1

was some kind of a god. And with his gun, with his finger on the trigger, with the slightest pressure now the difference between life and death, wasn't he like a god?

From far away the sound of a siren floated through the trees. The dog had started barking, jerking frantically at its chain. The skinhead had sunk to his knees, crying.

And the gun felt so powerful in Christopher's hand.

Zoey saw her mother's eyes were full of tears. She realized her own were, too. This was it—the destruction of her family. The end. Even worse, the destruction of her parents, all their tawdry, humiliating secrets now laid out to sicken their children. Zoey wished she could just disappear. If she'd still had even an ounce of energy or will, she might have grabbed Benjamin's hand and run. But all she could do was watch and listen, helpless to change anything.

"You might as well tell them the rest," Zoey's mother said flatly.

Mr. Passmore nodded. "Yes. The rest. It seems while I was with this woman in Europe, well, it seems she became pregnant."

Zoey felt the world spinning around her.

"See, you both, Zoey, Benjamin, you have . . . a sister."

Zoey Passmore

If I believed in astrology, I would have guessed that some terrible alignment of the planets occurred on that Thursday when so many futures stood teetering between happiness and destruction. Sometimes I wish I did believe in something supernatural, because then you'd have a way of making sense out of things, you know? Blame it on the stars or whatever, rather than having to blame people. Or yourself. But I was left feeling that life was just unpredictable, that it might suddenly, without warning, blow up in your face. Which isn't a very reassuring thing to believe, even though it may be true.

For me that Thursday
meant the end of my family
as I had known it. In the
blink of an eye my parents,
who I had been sure loved
each other absolutely, became enemies.

And each of them, my fa-
ther and mother, came away
seeming smaller, more petty,
weaker than I had believed.
Not that I had ever
thought of either of them as
perfect parents, but I
guess I'd always thought
of them as very good people
doing their best to be perfect parents, and that was
more than enough for me.
No longer.

It was like someone had
declared the end of illu-
sions. Illusions about
my boyfriend, Lucas, and
about Jake, my previous
boyfriend. And now my

parents. It made me wonder what other people I had misjudged. Nina had been my best friend for years, but if I could be so wrong about my parents, was I wrong about her, too? And Aisha? And even Benjamin, my brother, the one person I told myself was absolutely real?

And myself? Was I just a lie, too?

I sat in that room while my father told me the depressing truth and I had the strangest feeling. We were all still alive, my parents and my brother and me, tired, sad, but alive. And yet something had died.

Just an idea, really. The idea of a family. An abstraction. And it really shouldn't hurt when an idea dies, should it?

One

Sister. The word hung in the air between them. Zoey's mother looked away, her mouth twisted in a bitter line. Her father hung his head, ashamed.

"Where does this sister live?" Benjamin asked.

"I don't know," Mr. Passmore said. "Her mother and . . . and the man she thinks of as her father live in Kittery. I was never supposed to have anything to do with my—with the young lady."

"How *Montel Williams*," Benjamin muttered. "Or would this be more of a *Jerry Springer*?"

"I guess Lara—that's her name, Lara McAvoy—does know she has a biological father out there somewhere, but who, or where . . . I don't think she knows."

"This is not really what's important right now," Zoey's mother snapped in a brittle voice. Then, with an effort, she softened her tone. "The important thing is that you kids realize that both of us still love you and care for you. We don't want any of this to have to affect you."

Zoey laughed derisively. "Too late."

"Yeah, I think we kind of got affected," Benjamin said dryly.

"I'm just tired," Zoey said, shaking her head. "In a way I'm glad it's all out in the open."

Her mother leaned forward, trying to meet Zoey's evasive gaze. "What I said to you the other day, Zoey. About this being your fault. That was totally wrong. We're to blame. Your father and I, we're the only ones to blame."

Zoey stood up, wobbly with spent emotion and exhaustion. Outside, the night had fallen. Inside the room, no one had turned on more than a single dim lamp. Her parents' faces were in shadow, unknowable, almost unrecognizable in their masks of grief and shame and poorly concealed anger.

"Yes," Zoey agreed. "You are the ones to blame. But if you're waiting for forgiveness from me, Mother, you can forget it."

"People make mistakes," Benjamin said, so quietly Zoey wasn't sure she'd heard him.

"People make mistakes," Zoey agreed. "But they don't end up sleeping with men they're not married to on a tiny little island where everyone knows everyone else's business."

She was gratified to see her mother swallow hard. The barb had hit home. Good. They could say all they wanted that it was both their faults, but it had been her mother she'd walked in on. Her mother with Jake's father.

Zoey walked away. She heard Benjamin rise too and follow her from the room. Zoey began climbing the stairs, almost too exhausted to move her legs.

"Zoey?" Benjamin called out softly from the hallway.

She halted, waiting silently.

"People do make mistakes," Benjamin said.

* * *

7

The car swerved sharply around a cyclist, nearly invisible in the darkness, and fishtailed into a turn. In the backseat Aisha Gray was thrown against the door, bruising her narrow shoulder. But she didn't ask the driver to slow down. The speed of the car, now flying down the dark road, siren wailing, was Aisha's only hope.

"How do you know where we're going?" Aisha yelled at the detective on the passenger side, the older of the two men. Sergeant Winokur.

He half-turned, and Aisha could see that his eyes were wide from the adrenaline rush. They glittered with reflected green dashboard light. His voice, though professionally measured, showed the raggedness of excitement, maybe even fear. "We *don't* know," he said. "But there are three possibilities. I put units on the others, too, as soon as you told me what was happening."

Aisha was confused. "Wait a minute; you *know* who these guys are?"

Sergeant Winokur nodded. "We've known from the start. We have a pretty good idea who's in these skinhead gangs." He made an annoyed face. "Actually, we were hoping these particular lowlifes would lead us to bigger fish."

"Just ahead, Sarge," his partner said, killing the siren.

"Yeah. Look, miss, you stay in the car and keep down. Do you understand? Head below the back of this seat."

Aisha nodded. Her throat was tight. Her chest was a vise around a pounding, fearful heart. "Don't hurt him," she pleaded. "Just don't hurt him, please."

The sergeant gave no response. He tried unsuccessfully to hide the fact that he had drawn an automatic pistol from the holster beneath his sport coat. The gun was low by his side.

The car skidded to a stop, headlights illuminating a crazed, fleeting montage of dark tree trunks, a tilted mailbox, a gravel driveway, an old car, before coming to rest. Just up the street Aisha could see the van that Christopher had taken from the school's athletics department. She squeezed her hands together and prayed with all her might. Prayed like she had not done since she was a little girl.

"There he is."

"Yep."

Doors opened. Aisha looked up. Christopher walked blindly, head bowed, a stark figure in the blue-white glare of headlights. The gun hung loose in his hand. He seemed to be stunned, immobilized. He looked down at the gun, then up, straight into the headlights.

"Drop it." The sergeant rapped out the words. He stood behind the shelter of the open door, one foot still in the car, gun leveled at Christopher.

"Drop the damn gun!" the driver ordered.

Christopher still seemed confused, surprised, lost.

"I said lose the gun! Lose it right now or I'll shoot!"

Lucas's first kiss was tentative. Claire half-thought he might back away at the last minute. She half-thought *she* might back away, too. But neither did. And Lucas's lips met hers.

The betrayal was sealed. With that first kiss Claire had begun to pay Jake back for sleeping with Louise, for still secretly loving Zoey, and for the worst crime of all—for not really loving Claire.

But it wouldn't stop with one kiss. On the next

kiss Lucas was bolder, taking her in his arms and holding her close. The feel of him was different. Not like Jake, not the wall of hard muscle, the bristly chin, the sense of physical power barely restrained.

Nor was this Lucas like the Lucas that Claire remembered from a long time ago, when his kisses had been sweet, his touch so gentle. This Lucas was more urgent, almost harsh.

And yet Claire felt her body responding swiftly to his touch. Her lips, her throat as he trailed kisses down to her collarbone, her heart as it pounded frantically. It was as if her body was somehow a separate creature from her mind. She felt a warm, spreading, intoxicating pleasure, but at a distance, not real.

He drew back just a little, catching his breath. His face was too near for her to see his features distinctly in the dim light from the dashboard. He was a blur with warm breath and dark eyes. He came closer still, and this time she opened her lips to him, and felt an answering increase in his own excitement.

It was strange. Such a combustible feeling, as if the two of them brought together would inevitably cause an explosion. And yet it was a cold fire whose warmth reached just the surface of her skin, tingling just the nerve endings while somehow leaving her mind unaffected.

Was she the only one feeling this strange disconnection? Was it some consequence of guilt? Was it concern for Zoey, for Jake? Did Lucas feel it, too? Was that the reason for his urgency? Was he racing to stay ahead of feelings of guilt?

She fumbled for and found the control button that lowered the plush leather seat into full recline with a mechanical whir. Her luxuriant black hair fanned out across the tan leather. Guilt, maybe, but sheer pleasure, too. Lucas was over her now, his weight pressing down on her, kissing her deeply, the two of them panting, groping, unrestrained.

His hands touched her, eliciting shudders of sensual response. His movements were so barely controlled, his fingers trembling, his breathing ragged.

Why not? Claire wondered. It was very clear what he wanted to happen next. *Why not?* It was a wild, passionate, insane moment. How often did anything like passion infiltrate even the corners of her dispassionate mind?

And if Jake could do it with Louise . . .

Lucas was undressing her with hurried fingers, driven by desire . . . no, by two desires.

The second of which was to hurt Zoey.

"Sister?" Zoey repeated the word into the mirror over her dresser. "Half-sister," she corrected, but that formulation made her uneasy. She'd always felt there was something ungenerous about phrases like half-sister, half-brother. Like you were making an issue out of it. Like you didn't quite want to accept a person.

"I *don't* want to accept *any* of this." Her eyes showed the signs of sleeplessness and tears, the blue surrounded and invaded by redness, lids puffed, expression dull and lifeless. Her blond hair hung lank and straight to her shoulders. She glanced at her clock. Ridiculously early to get in bed. And yet when had she last had a real night's sleep?

She began to undress, letting clothing fall on the floor, feeling a deep physical craving for her bed. In a strange way she was almost relieved. Things became simpler when you were too exhausted to think. She could feel her mind finally shutting down, her

11

awareness like a diminishing circle of spotlight, smaller, smaller, releasing more and more into dark indifference.

She found her Boston Bruins jersey and slipped it on, reassured by its familiarity. At least some things didn't change. Her sheets were cool, her pillows soft. She stretched her legs out, feeling the tension in her every muscle. Her toes invaded the cold corners of her bed.

Her parents were breaking up. It was impossible to imagine that anything could stop the disintegration now.

And she had a sister, somewhere, maybe not far away, with no face as yet. An abstraction, but full of possibilities and problems that Zoey was simply too tired to contemplate.

Tomorrow she would have to begin confronting all the stories, the details, the trauma of this terrible day. But first . . .

. . . sleep.

Two

"Drop the damned gun!"

Christopher stood paralyzed. The bright light had come up from nowhere, and now voices were shouting. He looked down at the gun in his hand. It looked alien and alive. He opened his hand slowly and the creature slipped from his grip.

It was a shocking sensation, the emptiness of his hand, just fingers again. He shook his head, feeling like he'd been sleepwalking.

Strong hands grabbed him, a leg swept his feet from under him, and he was facedown in the gravel. Sharp rocks cutting into his cheek. Dirt in his mouth. His arms were twisted roughly behind his back. He didn't resist. He stared at the gun lying a few feet away, still more than just another artifact. Still like something living that had become a part of him.

Or was it the other way around? Was it he who had become a part of the gun?

He was jerked to his feet and pushed, staggering back against the hood of the car, blinking again in the lights.

"Christopher!"

Aisha. Her arms around him, her wet cheek

13

pressed against his. Was she crying? Was he?

"I'm making the weapon safe," a far-off voice said.

Sirens and wildly swinging blue lights were coming down the road at breakneck speed. One by one they skidded to a halt in a shower of gravel.

"This weapon has not been fired," the first voice said.

"Oh, thank God," Aisha said. "Oh, thank you, God."

"I couldn't do it," Christopher admitted, feeling embarrassed and defeated.

"Check around the back of the house," a second voice ordered. "I . . . Look, if the kid back there is in one piece, I don't need any formal statements from him at this time. You understand me?"

"Your call, Dave," the first man said, sounding doubtful.

"I couldn't do it," Christopher told Aisha.

"I know. I prayed so hard . . . I knew you wouldn't."

"I had him. I mean, he was scared, he was crawling and begging and all I had to do was pull the trigger—"

"But you didn't."

"I couldn't, Eesh."

Uniformed policemen were everywhere now. At least a half-dozen cars were spread out across and on both sides of the road.

The first cop was back. He jerked a thumb over his shoulder toward the dark backyard, back to the sound of a frantically barking dog and a high-pitched, almost hysterical voice crying for revenge, screaming obscene threats now that the danger was past. "He'll live. Just shaken up pretty badly."

"Any evidence of shots fired?" Sergeant Winokur asked.

"No shots. No witnesses aside from the victim and this clown." He indicated Christopher.

"All right, Curt, see if you can't break up this party while I have a little talk with the tough guy here. All right, tough guy, come with me," the sergeant said to Christopher. He hauled Christopher by his pinioned arm, pulling him, stumbling, down the dark road, away from the barking and the flash of blue lights and the wailing threats.

"Where are you taking him?" Aisha cried.

"See this?" the cop demanded angrily. "Do you see what you've done to this girl who cares about you? She has to call us and come racing over here scared half to death?"

Christopher shook his head in confusion. It was all happening in a blur. They were in darkness now, walking across dead leaves and fallen pine needles. A branch scratched his cheek. A sound was growing louder. Water. The river.

"Sergeant, what are you doing?" Aisha cried again, still keeping pace, clutching at Christopher's other arm.

They stopped beside the river, an almost unseen but definite presence, running fast and loud, swollen with new rain and too-early snowfalls melting off the mountains.

Christopher was turned around. There was a metallic click and suddenly his arms were free of the handcuffs. He was aware of the police sergeant standing no more than a foot away. He could feel Aisha wrapped around his right arm.

"That punk back there is named Jesse Simms. He was the third individual involved in the attack on you. Within about twelve hours of the incident, we'd rolled this kid over on his buddies. We've been trying to use the other two to identify additional members of this particular skinhead organization.''

"You knew?" Christopher asked.

"Yeah. Oddly enough, that's our job." The cop's tone was coldly sarcastic. "Sometimes we actually succeed. What was *your* job? What the hell were *you* doing here tonight with a gun?"

Christopher shrugged. "I . . . Look, they put me in the hospital, man."

"And the penalty for assault and battery is death now? Someone beats you up, you kill them? I'm curious, you know, since you're making all the laws now."

Christopher shrugged again. The sergeant was clearly angry and growing more so. Christopher felt too drained to say much in his own defense.

"So you were going to kill him," the policeman accused.

"He didn't, though," Aisha said fiercely.

"No. What he did was commit assault with a deadly weapon. We could probably also call it kidnapping since he held the poor bastard with a gun to his head. But I don't think Mr. Simms will be wanting to press charges, because I'm going to tell him not to."

Christopher exhaled and for the first time realized he had been holding his breath.

"So. Tough guy. Why didn't you shoot him?" the policeman asked more gently.

"I don't know."

"It would have been easy. You had the gun. He was helpless."

Christopher felt a wave of nausea at the memory.

16

Yes, he'd been helpless, crying, begging. "It made me sick."

"What made you sick? That he was scared? That he was begging for his life?" the sergeant bored in relentlessly.

"No," Christopher said sharply. "It made me sick that I made him beg."

"You enjoyed it. The rush of all that power from that little gun."

"No. Yeah, at first," Christopher admitted. "And then . . . Look, he deserved it. He's a racist piece of crap."

Surprisingly, the policeman laughed. "You know what? Lots of people deserve lots of things, kid. Sometimes they even get what's coming to them. Not all the time, but sometimes."

"And now what? Him and his friends will maybe spend ninety days in jail? Then it's right back out on the streets."

"That's about right."

"Maybe I should have killed him," Christopher said, but without conviction.

"And now you're ashamed because you didn't? You think you'd be proud if you had? You think you'd be standing here feeling like a big man because you took a life?"

"No," Christopher admitted.

"No. And you didn't get off on scaring that little punk. You know why? Because it takes a weak individual to enjoy causing fear. It takes a very small man to get pleasure out of another individual's pain. Maybe you just aren't a small enough man."

Christopher realized he was trembling, barely understanding what the cop was saying. All he knew was that a wave of relief so powerful it rattled him to his bones was sweeping over him. He had been so close to pulling that trigger.

Something was in his hand again. The gun. Emptied of shells, harmless, and yet so seductive.

"We checked you out after you first filed the complaint," Sergeant Winokur said in a quieter voice. "You work hard, kid. You have plans and you have a girlfriend here who is probably too damned good for you. And there was some provocation. So you're going to walk away from this one."

"Thank you," Christopher said in a whisper.

"Don't thank me," Sergeant Winokur said sarcastically. "I want a nice, clean case when we bust the rest of these punks. I don't want the jury having to deal with you playing vigilante. Now if you'd been found with a firearm, I wouldn't have much choice but to bust you and pretty much flush your life down the toilet. Do you follow me?"

"No . . . I . . ."

"What I'm saying is, that river is surprisingly deep way out in the middle."

Christopher nodded, comprehension penetrating his confusion. The sergeant gave him a long, thoughtful look. Then he turned his back deliberately and began to walk back toward the flashing blue lights.

"Thanks," Christopher called out after him. "I won't . . . you know."

There was no response. Christopher realized Aisha was still there, almost holding him up while his legs felt watery, his knees threatened to buckle. He felt weak as a newborn.

Aisha stepped away, waiting.

Christopher drew back his arm and found that he still possessed a reservoir of strength. The gun flew invisibly through the night. Seconds later there was a splash far out in the river.

"Let's go home," Aisha said.

"We can't do this, Lucas," Claire said a little breathlessly. "Not that I don't want to, but I think maybe it's a little far to take payback."

Lucas stopped his hand where it was but didn't pull it away. For a fleeting moment Claire wondered if he *would* stop. She had let things go way too far.

His voice was challenging. "That's all this is to you? Payback?"

"Oh, come on, Lucas, what is it to you?"

"It's . . ." He began cursing. He snatched his hand away, breaking contact.

Claire laughed. She used the button to raise her seat and began refastening everything Lucas had done such a good job of unfastening.

"You're cold, you know that?" Lucas demanded, sliding back across the seat.

"Uh-huh. I'm cold, but you've suddenly fallen madly in love with me, right? It isn't just that you're horny and you're mad at Zoey for refusing you. Or that you're worried about that long, very long hug between her and Jake? It isn't that you're thinking, 'well, I get laid, plus I get to pay Zoey back'?"

A semblance of humor returned to Lucas's features. "As revenge goes, it *would* be pretty effective."

"You and me. Could either of us have come up with a better way to piss off Jake and Zoey?"

Lucas laughed unwillingly, unable to resist the truth. "Still," he said ruefully, "it's not like I was just faking it."

"No, me neither," Claire admitted.

"You haven't exactly turned into a gorgon."

"We could definitely be dangerous together," Claire admitted. "But you're still in love with Zoey."

He shrugged and looked away.

"I think Jake is, too, at least partly."

Great, now she was feeling sorry for herself. Well, why not? Benjamin had obviously gotten over her a lot more completely than she'd ever expected. The level of affection between him and Nina was nauseating. And Lucas, and maybe even Jake, carried torches for Little Zoey Pureheart.

What did Jake feel for Zoey? What, if anything, did he feel for Claire? What, if anything, did anyone ever really feel for Claire?

Claire stole a glance at Lucas. Already the look of charged excitement was fading, replaced by a sober, worried expression. That worry was sure to grow. In a few minutes it would begin to occur to him that Claire now held his relationship with Zoey in the palm of her hand.

Claire turned the key in the ignition.

Claire

We all live on Chatham Island. Not a large island; in fact, it's small even by Maine island standards. Some maps don't even show it. It only has three hundred or so year-round residents. We get a lot more people in the summer, but the real, hard-core island population is just three hundred. North Harbor, which we jokingly refer to as our town, is really only a town when the tourists are in. Once September rolls around it starts to empty out, and by late October it's reduced to a few active businesses, a small grocery store that's only open a few hours a day, one year-round restaurant and bar, Passmores, which belongs to Zoey and Benjamin's

21

parents, a hardware store, and an automatic teller machine.

All of which is swell. Weymouth, which is a nice little full-service city, is just a half-hour ferry ride away, and from there we can always drive down to Portland or even Boston. But on a day-in, day-out basis I live on the island. And this can be a problem, because there is no natural camouflage in a community this small. There's none of that automatic invisibility you get in a real city, where no one knows anyone else and people on the street avoid making eye contact with each other. In a real city you can do what you want, and be what you want, and if you don't like what you were last week, you can just change to something new.

You can't do that on an island where everyone knows you and your family and where you live and probably what you had for breakfast. It places some limitations on you. Because, see, if you start trouble with another islander, it never entirely goes away. And likewise, if you fall in love with another islander, that never entirely goes away, either.

I live on an island where I have gone out with three of the four guys my age. Anywhere else it would be no big deal. But imagine you have one boyfriend now, and two ex-boyfriends, and every morning and again every afternoon, you find yourself on a ferry with them. And one of these ex-boyfriends is now going out with your sister, and another is now going out with one of your friends, and that friend used to go out with the guy you are now seeing. You can't develop a healthy hatred for your ex and just put him out of your life, because you're going to be seeing him every single day. So relationships never seem to completely die.

It tends to make you cautious in some ways.

Three

Claire and Lucas caught the nine o'clock, the last ferry back to the island, steaming away from the still-bright neon glow of Weymouth's restaurants and bars toward the darkened island, visible only as a few distant pinpricks of light.

Claire was surprised and a little disturbed to see Aisha and Christopher sharing the nearly empty deck. They were sitting toward the front, holding each other in a way that reminded Claire of the TV pictures of refugees. Something had gone wrong with those two on the mainland tonight, but whatever it was, Claire was pretty certain she didn't want to hear about it just now. At the moment she felt annoyed with herself, unsettled, and perilously emotional.

"Should we go back downstairs?" Lucas wondered in a whisper.

"Aisha saw us," Claire said. "It would look even more suspicious if we went below, or if we split up and sat on opposite sides of the boat. I mean, maybe we just both happened to be on the mainland for perfectly innocent reasons. That's how we should act, anyway."

"Cool. Besides, it's not like what we did was that big a deal," Lucas said.

"Yeah, you're right, Lucas. No big deal at all. You have half my clothes off and your tongue down my throat. No big deal." *Jerk*. She'd been planning to reassure him, but he was grinding on her nerves now. At least, something was grinding on her nerves. Probably just the after-effects of a strange week and a stranger evening.

Lucas looked around as if he was worried someone might have overheard. "Okay," he said in a low, urgent voice. "It was a big deal."

Claire rolled her eyes. "You know, your half of the human race is so pathetic sometimes."

"My half?"

"The male half. An hour ago you were all over me; now you're scared silly that Zoey will find out. You wanted to get laid so you could walk around all smug thinking, 'well, I guess I showed Zoey.' Except that one way or the other you don't want Zoey to really find out. Your hormones and your heart seem like maybe they're a little out of sync."

"You were in that car, too," Lucas pointed out. "You know, I'm not stupid, Claire. You enjoyed our little drive in the country as much as I did."

Claire shrugged in a show of nonchalance. "I enjoyed kissing you."

"Thanks, I guess."

"But it's like saying I enjoy ice cream or a nice hot bath. Physical pleasure is kind of thin and insubstantial and temporary, isn't it?"

Lucas looked thoughtful. "Yeah. I guess it's a bad idea to have a relationship that's purely physical. I mean, I guess."

"I don't know if it's good or bad," Claire said

impatiently. "But it's not going to happen. Not with me."

Lucas grinned. "What are you, Claire, some kind of secret romantic? You're holding out for true love and Mr. Perfect? Somehow I can't picture you that way. I always thought you were too . . . you know, too tough. I sort of pictured that when you decided to have sex, you'd just point at some good-looking guy and say 'Hey, you, come here.'"

"That's what you think?" Claire asked. "Is that really what you think about me?"

"Don't get bent, Claire, I was mostly kidding."

"Yeah, well, grow up," Claire said disparagingly. Of course it was what Lucas thought. It was what everyone thought. Claire could always take care of herself. Claire didn't need anyone. It's what Jake thought, too.

"I'm trying to grow up," Lucas muttered.

Claire resisted the urge to say more. The last thing she should do was open her heart to Lucas, of all people. But his neat caricature of her burned. Possibly because there was an element of truth to it. "You know what I think, Lucas? I think sex is easy. Any monkey, any cow, any pair of insects can have sex. Love is what's difficult."

"Sex doesn't seem to be all that easy for me," Lucas said wryly. "At least, not with Zoey. And even the love part . . . I mean, you're right, I do love her. But I feel like that's never enough for her."

"Zoey's an idealist," Claire said. "Zoey doesn't just believe in love, she believes it has to be perfect love. It has to be cosmic and flawless and unquestioning. See, people have always loved Zoey. Everyone loves Zoey. It's easy for her, so she's not interested in anything flawed or uncertain, where one

27

person maybe cares about someone and yet that person doesn't always show it the way she should. Zoey would never understand what it's like to be afraid that—'' She stopped herself cold. She had been twisting her fingers together in agitation. She had been on the edge of saying far too much.

Lucas waited. Then, in a newly gentle voice, he asked, "What doesn't she understand, Claire?"

What it's like to be afraid that no one will ever love her, Claire answered the question silently. But aloud she said, "Forget it, Lucas. Forget it, and forget this night ever happened. You can relax. I won't tell Zoey anything."

Lucas said good night to Claire at the ferry landing. She ignored him. She had raised her invisible shield and dismissed him as no longer being of any interest.

He wondered what it was that Claire had been looking for tonight.

He knew what he had been looking for, and now that the warm glow had worn off, that feeling was being replaced by a certain amount of disgust with himself. He had not been handling things well lately. First flying off the handle when Zoey had said no to . . . to moving their relationship to a new level. Then somehow (he wasn't sure exactly how) failing to make up with her, then *probably* overreacting to what was *probably* an innocent hug between Zoey and Jake, and now this exciting but definitely unacceptable make-out session with Claire.

God, it had been hot.

But wrong. Very wrong. Definitely wrong, and he was a pig.

Besides, it hadn't helped in the end. He didn't

love Claire, he loved Zoey. He was trapped, unable to escape. He loved Zoey. If he lost her, he wouldn't know what to do with himself. And yet at the same time, they had reached an impasse. He wanted to move their physical relationship forward, she didn't. Neither was prepared to give in. At least, he wasn't for long. And neither wanted the relationship to end. At least, he didn't.

He walked from the ferry through the silent streets alone. He had to pass Zoey's house on the way to his. He ought to stop by; it was only nine thirty and she wouldn't be in bed yet. Unless she would somehow guess what he'd been up to. Had Claire been wearing perfume that Zoey might recognize? What a disaster that would be.

So maybe it would be stupid to stop by Zoey's house. Besides, why should *he* crawl to *her*? She was the one who gave him that "I don't know" response when he'd asked her if she still loved him. She was the one who'd been treating him like crap lately.

Lately, as in ever since he'd told Zoey it was— do what he wanted or forget it. Ever since he'd trotted out that pathetic "Hey, look, if you won't, then there are lots of girls who will" line, sounding like some old, gold-chain-wearing, hey-baby-what's-your-sign bar lizard. He winced at the memory. Yeah, ever since *he'd* been a stupid, hormone-deranged jerk, *she'd* treated him like crap. And now he'd added to the mess by going behind her back and trying to get Claire to sleep with him. So now he could feel ten times as guilty, plus, he'd managed to get Claire pissed, too. Wonderful. He was certainly handling his love life well. Yes, he was a regular genius when it came to romance. Another week or two and he'd be about ready to join a monastery.

Maybe if he just went to Zoey, threw himself at her feet, and said "I confess, I'm scum, please forgive me and take me back." Maybe that would work.

Because, despite everything, he couldn't conceive of life without Zoey.

So he would crawl. He wouldn't confess everything; that would just be stupid, but he would crawl, beg, whine, plead, and if all else failed, squeeze out a few tears.

He turned the corner onto Camden and walked with renewed determination toward her house. "Zoey, I'm a jerk but I love you so please forgive me and take me back and tell me you love me too because otherwise—"

He came to a stop on the dark street. *Otherwise what?* he asked himself. Could she have really meant it when she said she didn't know if she still loved him? The pain of that thought pierced his heart.

No, of course she still loved him. She'd just been teaching him a lesson. Like he'd been trying to teach her a lesson with Claire tonight. But underneath it all, even if *she* was being bitchy and *he* was a jerk, there was still love. Wasn't there?

He had to find out. He started walking again, faster, determined. He had to find out because if the answer was no, then . . . well, what was he going to do then?

He looked up and saw her house, dark windows within darkness. His heart sank. Nine thirty and the whole place was dark? Since when did Zoey go to sleep this early?

Well, it wasn't like he could knock on the door and wake everyone up.

No.

But almost no one on Chatham Island bothered to lock their doors. And he knew about the squeaky stair. Third from the top, he was pretty sure.

He stood on the Passmores' front steps. He opened the door with painful care. Inside all was as dark as it had seemed. No TV, no stereo from Benjamin's room, just a deep silence.

Nine thirty and they were all asleep. What was that all about?

It was possible that going up to her room would just be another stupid move after a series of stupid moves. Very possible. But his mind was churning with a potent mixture of guilt and anxiety and still more guilt. He needed to talk to Zoey and find some reassurance.

He climbed the stairs like a burglar, stepping over the third step from the top, the one that squeaked. Barely breathing, he opened Zoey's bedroom door. Fortunately, he knew, she didn't sleep naked or anything.

What's fortunate about that? he asked himself wryly.

What's fortunate, he answered his own question, *is that when she jumps out of bed screaming hysterically, she'll get over it much faster if it turns out she's wearing clothes.*

He closed the door behind him. "Zoey?" A voiceless whisper. No response.

He went to her bed and knelt beside it. She was breathing in fits and starts, restless, as if she was having a dream. If she woke up screaming, he was going to have a very interesting time explaining this to Mr. Passmore. *Well, see, Mr. P., I was feeling guilty after making out with Claire, see, so I decided to sneak up here while Zoey was asleep and make sure she still loved me. Perfectly logical, Mr. Passmore.*

Did Zoey's father own a gun?

"Zoey?" A shade louder. She was heartbreakingly beautiful. Just the vision of her face, the face he loved, brought a lump to his throat. How could he have done what he tried to do with Claire? Because he was mad at Zoey? It seemed an inconceivably sleazy thing now.

He touched her hair, a tangle of shadows against the white pillow. Her forehead was damp with perspiration though the room was cold.

"What?" Clear, but uncomprehending.

"It's me, Lucas. Don't freak, okay?"

"Lucas?"

"Yes."

"What are you doing here?" Not angry, just confused.

"Kind of a long story," he whispered.

"I just had a terrible dream," she said, weirdly alert without sounding entirely awake. "My parents were getting divorced."

He stroked her forehead, feeling a fresh wave of tenderness toward her. "Just a dream, sweetheart."

She drew back, making room for him beside her. He slid into the bed, kicking off his shoes and shucking his coat. He could feel her warmth in the sheets. Zoey laid her head on his chest. Lucas wished his heart wasn't pounding so ferociously. For a while neither spoke.

"It wasn't a dream," Zoey said in a different voice.

"Of course it was."

She wrapped her free arm around him, holding

tight to his chest. The top of her hair, wispy blond tendrils, tickled his nose. "My dad is moving out tomorrow."

Was this still a memory of her dream? No, she was fully awake now. "God, Zoey," he said. "Is this . . . like, real?"

He heard her sniffle and realized she was crying. He began stroking her hair. Zoey's parents—Mr. and Ms. Passmore—getting divorced? No way.

And yet it might explain so much more. Had Zoey known this was coming? Was this the reason she'd seemed so distant these last few days?

"How long—when did you find out?" he asked.

"I don't remember. It's all just kind of . . ." The answer trailed away. "I'm very tired," she said. "I have to be asleep now."

"I'll leave," Lucas said. He started to get up.

But she didn't relax her grip on him, and after a while he heard her deep, regular breathing and knew that she was asleep.

Four

Nina Geiger looked up from the TV in the family room as the front door opened. She craned her neck to see, although she was pretty certain who was coming in. It wasn't like there were a lot of alternatives. Quickly she shoved a sketch pad she'd been drawing on under one of the throw pillows.

" 'Zat you?'' she yelled over the sound of the TV's laugh track, mumbling a little with the unlit Lucky Strike planted in a corner of her mouth.

No answer. Which meant it was definitely Claire. Nina fumbled around on the couch cushion, under the bag of no-fat and no-flavor-either potato chips. She found the remote control and muted the sound.

"Claire. I have to talk to you."

Claire appeared in the doorway. "Are you sure you have to?"

"Boy, you're getting home late," Nina said. "The coven meeting run long?"

Claire looked at her watch. "That makes five seconds of my time wasted. If you have something to say, get on with it. I'm tired."

"Okay, look," Nina said, trying to be conciliatory for once. "It's something I'm allowed to tell you. I mean, Benjamin said it was okay if I told you because it's not a secret or anything, but still you're not supposed to run around making a big thing out of it.''

"That's another ten seconds."

"Benjamin and Zoey's parents are splitting up," Nina said.

"What do you mean?"

"I mean, not to get into all the gross details, but it turns out both Mr. and Ms. Passmore are a lot more interesting people than anyone ever thought," Nina said. "Think *The Young and the Restless*. Think *As The World Turns*. I mean, Chatham Island *is* Genoa City."

Claire hesitated, obviously not convinced that Nina was telling the truth. She stepped into the room and, after a moment's more hesitation, sat in the easy chair. "Okay. You got me."

"This is totally serious," Nina said. "I mean, I really shouldn't be joking around, but this morning on the ferry Benjamin told me part of it, and then just a little while ago he called up sounding depressed and gave me the rest."

"Zoey didn't call?" Claire asked.

"No. But Benjamin and I talk about everything." It was true, and it gave Nina a little rush of satisfaction to be able to say it.

Claire curled her lip. "I never knew Benjamin to be so open about anything. You must have dragged it out of him."

"I guess he's open when he has someone he can trust," Nina said. Yes, it was a cheap shot, but then Claire had delivered a few to her over the years. Besides, a really cheap shot would have been telling Claire that Benjamin had finally said the three magic words. Throwing *that* in her face would be a cheap shot. It would be more fun if she saved that up for just the right moment.

"So the Passmores are separating," Claire prompted.

"Yes. Mr. P. is supposedly moving out tomorrow. They're going to keep the restaurant going for now, though."

"Why is this happening?"

Nina raised a suggestive eyebrow. "In a million years you'll never guess."

"Mr. Passmore forgets to put the toilet seat down?" Claire suggested.

"Funny. No, no, I told you—think soap opera. And Ms. Passmore is Erica Kane."

Claire stared at her. "Are we talking unfaithful?"

Nina nodded. Okay, she shouldn't be finding this juicy. After all, it was her best friend's and her boyfriend's parents. But Chatham Island was usually a pretty dull place and gossip like this didn't come along every day. "And guess who the other man is?" She said "other man" in a low, dramatic voice.

"Jeez, it's not Jake's father, is it?"

Nina was outraged. "How did *you* know?"

Claire shrugged. "Mr. McRoyan's that way. Everybody knows."

"I didn't. Besides, it was deeper than that. It turns out Mr. McRoyan and Ms. Passmore had a *thing* like nineteen years ago or something. This is back before the P's were married. Mr. P. takes a trip to discover Europe, and Ms. P. discovers Mr. McRoyan, who must have been cuter back then unless Ms. P. just has no taste. But, whoa, then Ms. P. discovers she's pregnant with none other than . . . our mutual friend Benjamin."

36

"By Mr. McRoyan?" Claire suggested, horrified.

"Nah. Although that would have added even more juice. No, Ms. P. is pregnant and Mr. P. is the daddy, so Ms. P. dumps Mr. McRoyan. Flash ahead nineteen years. Ms. P. discovers that oops, Mr. P. was discovering more than just Europe. He was also discovering a fellow American. He discovered her so much that *she*, this other woman, was also pregnant. In fact, she has a kid. Now Ms. P. learns this, is very pissed, decides it's payback time, and apparently ends up doing the nasty with Mr. McRoyan just as Zoey comes home early from Vermont."

"Payback." Claire nodded. She smiled her rare, wintry smile. "Awfully juvenile to think that sleeping with someone is a way to pay back your boyfriend."

"Husband."

"Right," Claire said, with an odd sardonic twist on the word. "Husband. Wait. This other woman was pregnant, too?"

"Give the girl a prize. It turns out Benjamin and Zoey have a half-sister."

"A half-sister by Mr. Passmore and some other woman. You're right, this is a soap opera," Claire said. "What's next? Someone's evil twin shows up? How is Benjamin taking this? Never mind, I forgot. Benjamin would never show any kind of real emotion over something this personal."

"He's pretty upset," Nina said. "He feels torn between his mom and dad, and also mad at both of them. But at the same time, he kind of looks at it as not being the end of life on this planet or anything. Mostly he worries about Zoey. She's the one who, you know, walked in on her mom and Mr. McRoyan."

"Benjamin told you that's how he feels, or you're guessing?"

"Of course he told me," Nina said.

Claire nodded. "Okay."

"I asked him if I should come over and be with Zoey, but he said no, everyone was exhausted."

"I can imagine," Claire said, sounding genuinely sympathetic.

"It's a major bum. I really liked their parents," Nina said.

"Liked, past tense? They're not dying, they're just getting divorced. Everyone does it." Claire's voice had caught on the word *dying*.

"Yeah, I know, but it sucks anyway. Especially for Zoey," Nina said, feeling a renewed sadness. It wasn't like anyone was dying, Claire was right. Not like *dying* at all. "You know Zoey," Nina said, trying not to let her thoughts veer where they had already veered. "She lives in a dream world. She never thinks anything bad is going to happen."

"Uh-huh. Too bad she doesn't have the firm grip on reality you have, living there inside your happy psychotic delusion."

The insult lay flat, without sting. Nina just nodded in acknowledgment. The details of the story might be juicy and even funny, but the effect they were having wasn't funny at all. Zoey must feel like she really was losing her parents in a way. And that was something that neither Nina nor Claire found at all funny.

"I hope Zoey's all right," Nina said. "I mean, you know. I guess it's kind of like it was when—" Damn. She shouldn't have gotten into this. Her eyes were filling with tears.

"Zoey'll be fine," Claire said softly. "Benjamin,

too. We survived, you know, losing um, you know, losing Mom, and . . . and, and that was worse than just being divorced.''

Nina smiled ruefully at her sister. ''Yeah, you can tell we survived fine by the way both of us are crying now.'' She squeezed her eyes shut and wiped the tears as they coursed down her cheeks.

''Tell Zoey and Benjamin if there's anything our family can do—''

''I remember when people were trying to be all nice to us.''

''I know. It didn't help. Nothing helps, I guess.''

Nina nodded agreement. ''But Zoey can handle it.''

At three A.M. Christopher's alarm went off. He hadn't been asleep more than a couple of hours, but he woke without resentment. He had work to do. The same work he got up for every day before the sun rose. A routine. It could be grueling at times, he often wished he could work less, but this morning the routine was sweet beyond imagination. To simply be doing what he always did. To be able to slip back so gratefully into his normal life.

So damned close to destroying everything. Another pound of pressure in his right index finger and his life would have changed forever. It was frightening how easily life could be taken and thrown away. It was like walking a tightrope, high in the air above the cheering crowds one minute and the next, with a single wrong move, a long, helpless fall.

He was going to have to watch the rope more closely in the future, to concentrate more on avoiding a mistake. Like losing Aisha. That was another mistake he had very nearly made. But she had come for him, trying to rescue him like the cavalry in an old movie, showing up at the very last minute with bugles blowing, horses at full gallop.

He made himself a pot of strong French roast coffee and fried some eggs. He needed the protein energy.

Outside, it was pitch black and dead quiet. Even the surf was subdued, barely surging over the sand. He climbed on his bike. He'd definitely have to buy an island car soon. It was getting way too cold to be pedaling around at three thirty in the morning.

He collected and divided his newspapers at the ferry landing. Weymouth papers, mostly, but also *Portland Press Heralds, Boston Globes*, and *Wall Street Journals*.

His last stop was always Gray House, the bed-and-breakfast Aisha's parents owned. It was the last stop because it involved a very tiring climb up the steep length of Climbing Way and he preferred to be rid of all unnecessary weight.

He leaned his bike against the fence and picked up the last papers. Ms. Gray had been extremely nice while he was recovering. Since then he'd been careful to set the papers precisely on the porch where no one even had to step outside to get them.

After placing the papers, he walked around the side of the big house to Aisha's bedroom window. It was dark, of course. She was asleep like any sensible person would be at this hour.

Still, it gave him a deep pleasure thinking of her safe and warm in her bed, just her beautiful face poking out from beneath the comforter. Her springy explosion of hair tumbled all around.

What kind of a fool had he been not to realize how great she was?

He went back around to the front, crunching pine needles underfoot and pulling up the collar of his jacket. The wind was always a bit stronger up here on the ridge.

He heard a soft click and looked to see the front door open, just a darker rectangle of shadow within shadow.

"Hi." Aisha's voice.

"Hi," Christopher said, flushed with excitement. He trotted over to her. She was wearing a long, sheer dressing gown and slippers.

"How are you doing?" she asked.

"I feel like a guy who miraculously survived a near-death experience," he said. "Like I was standing right in front of a speeding train and at the very last minute it somehow swerved and missed me."

Aisha laughed happily.

"I also feel like I've been the moron of the universe, in a lot of ways." He looked at her significantly.

"You have," Aisha said complacently. "But I can't stand out here and listen for as long as it would take you to make all the apologies you owe. I just thought you might be cold."

"I am a little," he said.

Aisha moved closer and put her arms around him. She kissed him deeply, then again, and again once more.

"Warmer now?" she asked.

"Much, much warmer."

"Good."

"Much."

Aisha smiled. "Do you have to cook tonight?"

"I'm supposed to, yes. Um, but afterward, I mean it's Friday night and all—"

41

"Okay. What do you want to do? It will be too late to take the ferry over."

Christopher sighed. "I know this will sound hopelessly dorky, but to tell you the truth, Eesh, I'd be happy if all I could do was just sit and look at you."

"That doesn't sound so dorky," Aisha said softly.

"You know, you got to kiss me, but I didn't get a chance to kiss you. And it would only be fair."

Aisha looked at him skeptically. "Is that how it works?"

"Uh-huh." He took her in his arms, holding her close, and kissed her. "Now we're even."

"Wouldn't want any unfairness," Aisha said in a voice that went from a squeak to a sudden throaty lowness.

"Tonight?"

"Tonight."

"And the next night?"

"Then, too."

Christopher rode away, possibly on his bike, although as he sped effortlessly down the long slope it felt like he might just be flying.

Police and Fire Log

BY DAN SMITH

Fire and rescue vehicles were dispatched to 1127 Pearl Street and successfully brought a kitchen grease fire under control. The residents had evacuated the building, and there were no injuries.

———————

Police units responded to a security alarm at Gifts by Terence, 809 Mainsail Street, and discovered that the premises had been broken into. Officers on foot gave chase to two young white males but were unable to apprehend them. Losses to the business included a broken window and a gift basket containing jams, cheese, and sausages.

———————

Police units responded to a disturbance at 4310 Brice Street involving two juveniles. Early reports that a gun was involved in the altercation proved to be false when a careful search revealed no weapons at the scene. No arrests were made.

———————

Fire and rescue vehicles responded to a call for medical assistance at The Breezes assisted-living facility. One person was taken to Weymouth Hospital emergency room with an apparent heart attack.

———————

Late last night Weymouth police units in concert with units from the state police rounded up a total of four members of the Aryan Defense Element, including two juveniles only recently released from state custody. A number of weapons were seized along with a quantity of hate literature. The Aryan Defense Element is a known white-supremacist gang originally thought to be based solely in Portland. The arrests came after several recent racially motivated attacks in the Weymouth area. Police sources say they acted on information from an informant within the gang.

———————

Fire and rescue vehicles responded to a 911 call stating that a person identified only as "Charles" had climbed a tree and was in danger of serious injury. Units arriving on the scene retrieved Charles—an orange tabby cat—and returned him to his owner.

LUCAS CABRAL

For a guy, life is always, about having to do things you don't want to do and not being allowed to do things you do want to do. Maybe it's that way for girls, too. I don't know, not being one. But for a guy it's always—be tough, be brave, be manly, never show one minute of weakness because if you do, you're marked for life. You act weak or pathetic and it's like someone might as well tattoo the word victim on your forehead because that's what you are from then on. Sometimes it would be nice not to have all that pressure. It might be nice to just once, when something terrible happens, be allowed to start blubbering and weeping and running around all depressed. But what you have to do is kind of shrug it off. Play through the pain, as all the jocks say.

And at the same time,

everything you do want, you're not allowed to have. Can't drink, can't smoke, can't do drugs, can't have sex. The first three I can live without. But the truth is, number four does kind of occupy your mind when you're a guy. It occupies it the way . . . well, did you ever hear about the Donner Party? Those people who starved to death in the mountains back in the old west days, and it got so bad they ate their relatives? You can imagine how often they thought about food? That's how often I think about sex.

So here's the deal. Your girlfriend wants you to be sensitive and open and understanding and never to pressure her, but if you do all that, then guys think you're a wuss. Besides, if you ever honestly tell a girl what's on your mind, she'll think you're a pervert. So you have to be somewhat open and mostly honest

with girls, but not ever let
other guys find out. Which, when
you think About it, is fairly
insane.

I try to kind of walk the line.
I mean, I truly love Zoey, And
it makes me feel good when I
can talk to her And tell her how
I feel About things. But At
the same time, I have to be
tough. I can't just let her
make All the big decisions.

I think girls have it easier.
Maybe not, but it seems that
way.

Zoey

I've often thought it would be great to be a guy. Not that I am in any way unhappy being female. I am glad I'm a girl. I'm just saying it's easier being a guy, especially in relationships. It's like they have so much less to think about and worry about. For them it's so much about just having sex. I mean, it must be nice to have everything reduced down to such a simple perspective, you know? No complexities or worries, really. Just on this mission to have sex. Night and day.

Okay, yes, I know I'm exaggerating, but it's like, when you're a girl, things are complicated right from the start. The biggest difference is that we can get pregnant, so it's not just like, hey, sex is another form of entertainment. I've heard guys-not Lucas, but guys I've known-say sex should just be another fun thing to do on a Saturday night, like seeing a movie or shopping. I don't know if they really believe that or just say it to sound tough and cool for their friends. Probably they wish it were true. Only going to see a movie doesn't result in you getting pregnant or catching a disease. So, see, there is that little difference.

You mention this to a guy and he just shrugs and goes, uh, well, I'm on a mission to have sex because I have all these hor-

mones. Plus I have to do it
or my friends will think
I'm lame. See, it has to be
easier being a guy and getting to just think about
all the fun aspects of
things without having to
get all serious and de-
pressing with the reali-
ties.

In a way I feel like guys
get to be kids longer than
girls. It's like we have to
grow up faster, which
sucks.

Five

Zoey was first aware of the fact that her radio alarm had gone off. The music was Redd Kross, singing "It's a crazy, crazy world we live in." Zoey was next aware of the fact that her pillow seemed unnaturally hard and was rising and falling slowly.

She opened her eyes and was surprised beyond belief to discover Lucas, arm crooked back behind his head, the pillow of his chest rising and falling slowly. There was a little wet spot on his shirt where she had drooled.

He stirred, one eye blinking open, shutting, then both eyes opened suddenly.

"What am I doing here?"

"That's just what I was wondering," Zoey said. She realized one of her legs was still entwined with his and quickly disentangled herself. "How did you get in here? Am I awake?"

"Oh." He sat up, wincing in pain, and rubbed at his neck, which he held forward at an odd angle. "I just came by to see you last night. You fell asleep on me."

"I did?" That didn't seem likely, but she did have a vague, dreamlike memory of something . . .

"Yeah, remember? You told me about, you know, about your folks."

"Oh. Right." Zoey tried self-consciously to push her hair into some kind of recognizable shape. Her folks. Yes, for several seconds she'd managed to forget about that. She hoped Lucas wouldn't notice the wet spot on his shirt.

"You look beautiful in the morning," Lucas said, smiling in spite of the fact that he couldn't sit all the way up.

"No, I don't." Another halfhearted attempt at straightening her hair. She kept her distance in case she had dread morning breath.

"Actually, you do." He looked around the room, twisting his neck and grimacing. "I guess I'm wearing my same clothes to school. I can sneak out past your parents if you look out for me."

"You don't have to sneak," Zoey said quickly. "I don't care what my parents see. They have no right to tell me how to live my life."

Lucas raised his eyebrows but said nothing.

The radio reminded them both that it was a crazy, crazy world.

Zoey smiled ruefully. "I know I sound like I'm being bitter, but that's not it. I'm just growing up. I've just figured out some stuff."

"They're still your parents," Lucas said with a diffident shrug.

"They're Jeff and Darla," Zoey said dismissively. "I have an extra toothbrush if you want."

"Really? You keep a supply, do you?"

"I always switch to a new one every month, so I have next month's still in its little box. Now you've learned one of my deep, dark secrets. It's pink," she added apologetically. "I change colors every month, too."

Lucas nodded. "Probably floss every day, too."

"Twice, actually."

"Well, I approve of good oral hygiene."

"Um, Lucas?" Zoey asked hesitantly.

"What?"

"Are you . . . you didn't take off your pants or anything, did you?"

Lucas grinned and threw back the blankets. Zoey saw wrinkled Levi's.

"You slept all night in jeans and your shirt and me crushing you?" She ran her fingers through his matted hair, an even bigger mess than hers.

"I didn't want to wake you up. You seemed very tired. You fell asleep instantly. Like a light switch."

"I was exhausted. I haven't slept in a long time, with all this stuff going on." She looked at him closely. "I've probably been a jerk to you lately."

He smiled sheepishly. "It's okay. I was a bigger jerk." For a moment he looked like he had something else to add, but he said nothing.

Zoey looked thoughtfully around the room. Sunlight forced its way around the edges of the shade. In the dormered window where she had her desk, she noticed the bare side walls. Normally they would have been cluttered with Post-it notes bearing her favorite quotes. But she had thrown them all away. Along with the journal where, over the years, she had written the first chapter of her romance novel more than twenty times. And the journal her mother had kept, starting with Zoey's birth and up through all her subsequent birthdays. All gone in a cleaning out of memories of things now past.

She felt sad, despite the sunlight. Today her father

was moving out of the house. She wondered if she should skip school, stay home and help somehow. But was that the right thing? What exactly was the correct protocol when your father was leaving his home?

As if he'd read her mind, Lucas asked, "Are you going to school today?"

Zoey sighed. "If I stay home, I'm afraid I'll just make things worse. My dad—" Her words were choked off by a rising lump in her throat.

Lucas took her hand and held it in his lap.

"He's moving out," Zoey said. "Maybe I should help him. Only I'll just end up crying and being mad. And I feel like, I don't know, like I'm just halfway sane right now and I don't want to go back into all that. You know?"

"Yeah, I know. You have to keep yourself together in all this."

"Maybe I'm just being a coward."

Lucas shook his head. "This will be bad for your father, too," he said. "You think he wants to have to do this with you watching and crying the whole time?"

"But I can't stand the idea of him walking out of here, out of a silent house with no one even to say good-bye." She brushed wretchedly at a tear. "Damn, that's enough. I've cried enough."

Lucas started to put his arms around her, but she held him back. "Don't, please, or I'll just lose it completely. I have to get out of this house," she said with sudden decisiveness. "I can't be here today. I can't, I'm sorry."

"Sometimes I feel myself slippin', but I guarantee you I'll never fall. . . ."

Benjamin had a world-class stereo system and didn't have to rely on radio potluck to wake him up. The CD he'd picked and programmed the night before came on at the appointed hour on the chosen cut, and Clarence "Gatemouth" Brown and his guitar sang out from speakers around the room and in his adjoining private bathroom.

He knew it was kind of a cliché that a blind person would turn to music, but even if it was just a compensation for the lost world of sight, it still wasn't a bad compensation. His CD collection, all neatly arranged in racks, labeled in his own Braille stickers, covered the whole range of music from baroque to opera to big band to rock to blues. About the only thing left out was country, unless you counted Lyle Lovett and Patsy Cline.

This cut ran about six minutes, during which he climbed out of bed, wearing only a pair of boxers, brushed his teeth, ran the electric razor over his face (not that this was strictly necessary every day), and climbed into a regrettably cool shower. Zoey had beaten him to the hot water again.

"Nobody but nobody can have good luck every day," Gatemouth pointed out wisely.

Benjamin raced the rapidly diminishing hot water, rinsing finally in something barely above ice water.

He half-dried himself and ran for warm clothing, shivering and cursing under his breath. But a surprising number of his hangers were empty. In fact, it would take some searching to put together anything like a normal outfit. Fortunately, he kept his clothing options limited, sticking to dark browns, dark blues, grays, and blacks, with the occasional plaid shirt. That way he was less likely to end up wearing something bizarrely mismatched.

He and his mother had worked out a system with the hangers so he could manage it all himself without the humiliating need of asking someone to pick his clothes for him.

Oh. Of course, he realized. No wonder the closet was nearly empty. His mother had been a little preoccupied these last few days.

He felt a momentary annoyance, but fought the impulse to get angry. It was pretty irrelevant, really. Although it could be seen as an omen of things to come. It was the kind of thing that reminded him that no matter how well he coped, he was still dependent in some things. He still couldn't separate whites and colors to do a load of wash; a minor, silly thing to worry about, but still . . .

"Stop it, Benjamin," he ordered himself. He was treading too close to self-pity, and that was definitely not allowed. He found his remote control and replayed the same song. He sang along with the music. "Sometimes I feel myself slippin', but I guarantee you I'll never fall. I hold my head up high and wade through water, mud and all. . . ."

"You will never be a blues singer," Benjamin admitted. "Just too damned white."

There was a tapping on his door.

"Come in." He muted the music.

"It's me." His mother.

"Hi."

"Look, Benjamin, I thought maybe we should have a little talk."

"Okay. But I don't have much time before I have to head for the ferry."

"So you . . . you *are* going to school?" She sounded surprised.

"That was the plan," he said. "It's a school day."

"I thought maybe you'd feel like you had to stay home. You know, for your father." Her voice quavered.

Benjamin shrugged. "If I thought I could help, I guess I would. Is that what you wanted to say? You want me to stay home today?"

"No. Just the opposite. I was going to tell you that you should go to school. I think you and Zoey both need normalcy now, as much as possible."

"Did you talk to Zoey?"

A long pause. "No. I don't know that Zoey would listen to much I have to say. I think she's very, very angry at me."

"Gee, I can't understand why," Benjamin said sarcastically. He instantly regretted his tone. He didn't want to get angry. And he didn't want to hurt either of his parents. They were already doing a good job of that themselves.

"Anyway," his mother said heavily. "I wish you'd make sure Zoey goes today, too."

"I don't tell Zoey what to do." Despite his best efforts he was beginning to get annoyed. His mother was just grinding him the wrong way.

"You *are* her big brother."

"I'm two years older and still in the same grade," Benjamin pointed out.

His mother wasn't making it easy for him to maintain his calm. She really should just go away now. She really should let him just finish dressing and getting ready to get the hell out of this house.

"That's not through any fault of yours, Benjamin. You know, I guess in some way you're going to be the man of the house—"

"Shut up," Benjamin snapped, suddenly viciously angry. "Just shut up. My father is *the man* of this house. I'm not *the man* of a damned thing. I'm a nineteen-year-old guy who's trying to get through twelfth grade without being able to see a blackboard or read half the books. I'm smart enough to just about manage it. And I'm clever enough to make people like me instead of laugh at me, and treat me like an equal instead of punching me out for the sheer hell of it, and isn't that wonderful. I'm Benjamin the Blind Wonderboy. But that's all I can handle, Mom, so don't dump your problems on me and start telling me I'm *the man* around here, whatever the hell that's supposed to mean."

"Sorry. I meant it as a compliment."

"Great. I'm flattered. I have to finish getting ready for school."

"This isn't easy for me, either, you know," his mother said.

Benjamin unmuted the music. His hand was trembling.

"Nobody but nobody can have good luck every day. . . ."

Six

Lucas tore at the stubborn wrapping of the toothbrush, finally got it open after some muttered curses, and applied toothpaste. He had been in Zoey's bathroom before, but never this early in the morning and after having just spent the night sleeping with Zoey.

Sleeping with Zoey. That had a nice sound. Sleeping with Zoey. Yep, a very nice sound.

He realized he was grinning at his reflection in the bathroom mirror. *Just* sleeping, he reminded himself, which wiped the smile away.

Still, it seemed like they were back on more normal terms, Zoey and him. She'd sort of apologized for being hard on him, and now that he knew what had been going on with her, he could forgive very easily. If only she'd told him earlier. Only, of course, they'd been fighting, so naturally she hadn't told him. But if she *had*, then he wouldn't have been so upset, and he would have understood *why* she had been acting way too friendly to Jake. After all, his father was involved in the whole divorce mess, too. If he'd known all that . . .

Damn. He froze, looking at his suddenly pale reflection. If only he'd understood all that, he wouldn't have gone off with Claire and made out and tried to do a whole lot more. The memories came back sharp and clear. And with the memories came two feelings. One was definitely guilt. The other was, unfortunately, a kind of lingering excitement. Which led directly back to guilt.

Okay, so he had gotten some superficial physical pleasure out of making out with Claire. Obviously. She was a beautiful, sexy . . . cold-blooded, ruthless, almost reptilian girl. Who now had the power to destroy his fragile relationship with Zoey anytime she wanted to just by opening her mouth. A relationship that, even with all its frustrations, was the most important thing in his life.

He spit and rinsed. "She won't say anything," he muttered to the wary-looking face in the mirror. No. He could trust Claire.

Yeah, right. Oh, certainly he could trust Claire.

He opened the bathroom door and peeked out. The coast was clear. He dashed quickly to Zoey's room.

"Ready?" she asked.

He made an exaggerated smile, showing off his sparkling teeth. "Now is it time for a morning kiss? I think it should be a regular thing we do whenever we sleep together."

Zoey smiled halfheartedly, and followed it with an equally halfhearted kiss. "Let's go or we'll miss the ferry."

"Hey, are we going out tonight?" Lucas asked. "I mean, I guess you wouldn't want to, probably."

"No," Zoey said. "I won't feel like going out tonight."

Lucas tried not to look disappointed, but he must not have been too successful because Zoey put her arm through his and gave him a kiss on the cheek.

"How about tomorrow night?" she said.

"Saturday night! Absolutely."

They tramped down the stairs and ran into Benjamin in the entryway. Zoey winced, obviously embarrassed at having to explain to her brother why her boyfriend was there.

Lucas held a finger up to his lips. He fell into step as silently as he could behind Zoey and Benjamin. After a few minutes he'd say hi to Benjamin, like he'd just walked up.

"Hey, Zoey," Benjamin said.

"Good morning, Benjamin," Zoey said.

"You know, Zoey," Benjamin said as they set off down the street, "I've been thinking over what you said the other night; you know, about how Lucas is probably just overcompensating for feelings of inadequacy as a male and possibly even latent homosexuality? I think that may be true."

Lucas made a disgusted sound. "Okay, very humorous."

"Like I can't tell the difference between one person coming down a flight of stairs and *two* people," Benjamin said cockily. "Like I can't hear your big galumphing boots. And not to be cruel, but someone here didn't shower this morning."

"He came over early," Zoey said.

Benjamin shrugged. "I'm not Mom or Dad. Come to think of it, Mom and Dad aren't exactly Mom and Dad anymore. Did Zoey tell you about the Passmore scandal?"

"Yeah," Lucas said. He felt very uncomfortable being part of a conversation about their parents. He had always genuinely liked Mr. and Ms. Passmore. In fact, Zoey's family, living in what had seemed like idyllic family bliss just down the hill from his own screwed-up family, had always been a kind of example of how things could be. *Might* have been, if his own father weren't a tyrant and his mother too weak to resist him.

"I told Nina, too," Benjamin said.

"How did she take it?" Zoey asked.

Benjamin smiled, a sweet, tender expression. His voice, which had been hard and cynical, softened by several shades. "She was fine. You have excellent taste in best friends, Zoey."

Lucas and Zoey exchanged a look. Lucas looked quickly away. The image of Nina in his mind was replaced by the image of Claire.

Claire. Guilt mixed with memories of pleasure, followed by dread. Claire wouldn't say anything, he told himself again. Why would she?

"Did you see Mom or Dad this morning?" Zoey asked Benjamin.

"Mom. We kind of got into it. She wanted me to talk you into going to school today."

Zoey nodded and shot an embarrassed glance at Lucas.

"You guys want me to leave?" Lucas volunteered. "I mean, you know, family stuff and all."

"No, no," Benjamin said. "We're not going to have a big talk or anything. Tell you the truth, I'm sick of the whole subject."

"I'm going to go see Dad after school," Zoey said. "Find out where he's staying and maybe bring him something. Cookies or something."

"I guess that would be a good idea," Benjamin said. "Maybe I'll go with you. I want to find out about this girl. This half-sister."

Lucas looked quizzically at Zoey. Zoey looked

down at the ground. Benjamin stopped, sensing this new tension.

"Zoey, there's no point in trying to keep that secret," Benjamin said. He turned his sunglasses in Lucas's general direction. "Turns out our father has supplied us with a half-sister."

Lucas had absolutely nothing intelligent to say to that piece of news. Zoey and Benjamin had a half-sister? It was starting to seem like he'd been wrong about the Passmores being so normal.

"Whoever she is, she means nothing to me," Zoey said. "That all took place a long time ago, before I was even born. Dad wasn't much older than we are now when it happened. At least when *he* screwed up he was young, unlike Mom."

"Zoey, don't get into choosing sides between Mom and Dad," Benjamin said.

Lucas had begun to feel extremely uncomfortable.

"What Daddy did happened nineteen years ago," Zoey said coldly. "What our mother did happened last week. Don't forget, I saw it. It was . . . Look, she betrayed Dad, you, me—" Her eyes were hard in a way that Lucas had never seen before. "I don't like sneaking and secrets and betrayal."

Lucas sucked in a deep lungful of air. He put his arm around Zoey, comforting her, feeling her angry trembling.

Sneaking and secrets and betrayal. He replayed the phrase over in his mind. Yes, sneaking. Yes to secrets, too. And a betrayal that would have been a lot worse if Claire hadn't put a stop to things.

Claire would keep quiet, he told himself. Because if she didn't, it would be the end of the one real love in his life.

Seven

"It's the big line of goo," Nina announced with some satisfaction as she surveyed the length of the cafeteria line. "More goo per square foot than has ever been brought together in one place. The home office of goo. Goo central. Warm goo, cold goo, goo the temperature of spit. Wait, that *is* spit. Goo with and without sauce. It's a celebration of goo. A monument to goo."

"So you're saying *goo*?" Benjamin asked tolerantly.

"Well, the main course today seems to be paste studded with bits of dog food."

"That's the Friday special," Benjamin agreed.

"The vegetable is green, but the bad news is, it's carrots."

"But seriously, folks." Benjamin laughed, and Nina felt that semi-delirious feeling that came over her all too often when she was with Benjamin lately. Something between the early symptoms of flu and the giddy-moronic feeling when her dentist gave her nitrous oxide. Objectively speaking, it was basically an unpleasant feeling, except that it was intensely pleasurable.

He was just behind her in line, and when she stopped for the person in front of them, he bumped into her. She bumped back, playfully, and the half-sick feeling just got worse. Or better. She accepted a plate from the cafeteria ladies.

"Yours is up," she told Benjamin. "About two inches left. Just follow the smell."

He retrieved his plate and again bumped into her. This time Nina had stopped suddenly for no reason except that she wanted him to bump into her. *Very juvenile*, she scolded herself.

They were at the end of the line. This was one of the few places where Benjamin could actually use a hand. He could negotiate a lot of things using his remarkable memory, but the configuration of the lunchroom changed every day.

She guided his hand to her arm and led him to an empty table. As soon as Benjamin sat down, two sophomore girls sat down nearby, looking far, far too innocent to be innocent. Nina gave them a dirty look. Then she glanced over to her usual table. Zoey, Aisha, and unfortunately, Claire.

"Maybe I'll sit with you today," Nina said.

"You know I'd love that," Benjamin said. "But I don't think you should mess with tradition."

"Yeah, tradition," Nina said unenthusiastically. She and Zoey and Aisha and sometimes Claire had been eating lunch together for years, uninterrupted by boyfriends for the most part. She'd thought it was a great idea back in the days when she was the only one without a boyfriend. "Well, there are two girls here at the table to talk to. A pair of sophomores, and only one of them has really bad leprosy."

Benjamin laughed again, and the two girls gave Nina cold stares.

"Hey, we're going out tomorrow night, right?" Benjamin asked.

"Sure. Not tonight?"

Benjamin sighed. "I don't think so. Zoey and I are going to see our dad at his new location."

Nina winced. "Ouch."

"Yeah. But tomorrow? I mean, if you can spare the time. It's Richie Felix's birthday party."

Nina grinned. "I totally forgot. Richie's birthday party. Remember last year when Melanie Amos hit that guy over the head with a bottle like she thought she was in a cowboy movie or something and he had to go get stitches?"

"And how many major boyfriend-girlfriend fights were there?" Benjamin asked. "I mean, I'm only counting ones where objects were thrown."

"Too bad Richie's such a strange kid. He has the world's most bizarre parties."

"You and I calling someone strange?" Benjamin said.

"Yeah. Well, your food's getting cold and that isn't going to help."

"Okay, sweetheart. I'll see you later."

Nina leaned over and put her mouth beside Benjamin's ear. "I have to tell you a secret."

"What?" he whispered back.

"I love you."

"I love you, too," he said.

That stupid feeling was back, and Nina realized she was grinning like the kind of sappy little dip who made her sick. If she'd been looking at herself right now, she'd roll her eyes and make some smart, cutting remark. But it wouldn't matter, she realized, because when you were in love it didn't matter what anyone else on earth thought or said, because pretty much everyone aside from Benjamin had temporarily ceased to exist.

"I am making myself sick," she muttered under her breath as she reluctantly carried her tray toward her usual table. She wiped the grin off her face and adopted a very cool expression that gave nothing away.

She took the seat between Claire and Zoey. Claire was shaking her head in disgust. Both Aisha and Zoey were batting their lashes at her.

"What?" Nina said grouchily.

"She's beaming again," Aisha told Zoey.

"Eyes shining, dopey grin, face red," Zoey confirmed.

Nina scowled. "What are you guys talking about?" She took a cigarette from her purse and planted it, unlit as always, in the corner of her mouth.

"Yeah, the cigarette is sure to hide that dweeby grin," Aisha said, rolling her eyes.

"I never thought I'd have to use the word 'Nina' and the words 'aww, isn't that sweet' in the same sentence," Zoey said.

"I'm not at all surprised to have to use the word 'Nina' and the words 'I may throw up' in the same sentence," Claire said. "Can we get past this and go on to the next step—Nina's daily ritual of abusing the food?"

"Funny you should ask," Nina said, glad to have the subject changed. She fumbled in her book bag and produced a sketchbook. She opened it to a black line drawing and shoved it in front of Claire.

Claire nodded thoughtfully. "Well, now I'm all the way sick." She pushed her food away. "You know, I'll never get fat as long as you're around, Nina. It's like a diet, almost."

Aisha grabbed the sketchbook, looked it over, and laughed.

"I'm thinking what I'll do is Xerox off like a hundred copies and spread them around the cafeteria Monday," Nina said, laughing at the possibilities.

"You know, that's a sickening cartoon," Aisha pointed out, "but it's kind of good, too."

"It is good," Zoey confirmed. "Since when do you draw?"

"It's just a little cartoon." Nina shrugged. "Any idiot could draw it."

"And one idiot did," Claire said.

"No, not *any* idiot could draw it," Aisha argued.

"No, you're right, it would take a particular idiot," Claire agreed.

"I'm serious," Aisha said.

"You know what you ought to do," Zoey said. "You should take it to Mr. Schwarz and see if he'll put it in the school paper. We're short this week. I'd talk to him for you, but I'm not exactly his favorite student right now."

Nina knew Zoey had recently refused to do a story on drug use by the football team, because the story would have implicated Jake. And since it had just been one incident, Zoey had argued it wasn't a real story.

"I thought your teacher agreed it wasn't enough of a story," Claire said. *Still looking out for Jake*, Nina noted.

"He did, but he's still pissed," Zoey said. "He thinks I was influenced by the fact that I care about—" She paused, swallowed, and backed up. "I mean, that I used to care about Jake." She

quickly turned her attention back to Nina. "But I'm serious, Nina. You should show that to Mr. Schwarz. We've never had a cartoonist in the paper."

Claire colored and concentrated on her food.

"Maybe I will," Nina said. She gave Claire a triumphant look. "Then I won't just be an idiot, I'll be a published idiot."

But there was no answer from Claire. Claire's eyes were far away. An expression that, in anyone else, Nina would have taken for sadness.

Jake fell in beside Zoey as she climbed the stairs from the cafeteria up to the second floor for their English class. She was walking alone, looking distracted, lugging her books and notebooks like they were a great weight.

"Hey, Zoey," he said, taking the steps two at a time to catch up with her.

She paused and waited for him, leaning against the rail to stay out of the flow of kids going up and down, a thin, almost fragile figure to Jake's eyes, her wispy hair as usual not quite forming any recognizable style.

He felt an urge to touch her, to hold her hand, but resisted. Things weren't that way between them, not anymore.

"Hi, Jake," she said, forming a smile.

Suddenly he felt almost bashful, at a loss for words. "I was just . . . I just wanted to check and see if you were okay."

"I'm doing okay. My dad's moving out of the house." Her lip quivered, but she overcame the emotion. "He's always saying he can't get to sleep because there's too much noise from all of us, so I guess it will be good for him."

Jake nodded. "I'm sorry to hear that. I always liked both your folks."

"Me too. I mean, your parents. Did anything—?"

He shook his head uncomfortably. "No. My mom is one of those people who doesn't ever hear anything or see anything she doesn't want to see, you know? Besides, she's not like your mom. She'd be totally lost on her own. What can she do aside from bake pies? Your mom is so much more independent. Maybe that's why my dad—" He waved the thought aside. It was just too gross to get into the whole question of why his father and Zoey's mother would end up having an affair. He knew there was supposedly a history there, going back to a long time ago, but they were the people they were today, and it wasn't nineteen years ago. It was now.

Zoey reached out and put her hand over his. It was a perfectly innocent gesture of comfort for a friend, Jake believed, but there were two facts that made that belief hard to sustain. First was the fact that the touch had a profound effect on him. Second was the fact that Claire chose that moment to pass by. Her dark eyes were cold and accusing, and Jake responded by jerking his hand away guiltily.

"Claire!" he called out.

Zoey turned, flushing pink.

A rushing group of freshman guys obscured Claire for a moment. Then she stepped forward with a look in her dark eyes that would have made Jake take a step back if he hadn't already been pressed against the railing.

"Hi, Jake. Hi, Zoey. Is this a closed meeting of the mutual support society?"

"I was just asking Zoey if . . . if she was okay," Jake said.

"And is she?" Claire asked. The words were silky, but cracked like a whip.

Jake nodded.

"Good," Claire said. "And have you checked with Louise Kronenberger lately to see if she's okay, too?"

Jake flushed. He wasn't easily intimidated, but Claire was capable of an ice-cold fury that was just scary. In a part of his mind he couldn't help but admire her. "Not lately," he said.

"Too bad, because I like to make sure absolutely everyone is okay. Zoey, Louise, Lucas." She turned on Zoey. "Is Lucas okay, too?"

Zoey was blushing darkly, her face set in resentment. "Yes, he's okay," she said through gritted teeth.

"Just okay?" Claire demanded. "I'm a little surprised. I found him much, much better than just okay."

Claire hadn't meant anything by it, Zoey told herself for the thousandth time in an hour. All through English, Claire's snide remark had distracted and bothered Zoey. Which was probably just what Claire had intended. Claire had seen her touching Jake, and she obviously wasn't ready to tolerate any unfaithfulness on his part.

Well, Zoey could hardly blame her. Infidelity wasn't her favorite human failing right now, either.

So Claire had taken a shot. It hadn't meant anything. How could it have?

Maybe she was referring back to the old days when she and Lucas were girlfriend and boyfriend. That was probably it.

71

Besides, when would there have been time or opportunity? Unless . . . had Lucas been on the afternoon ferry Thursday? No. She didn't think so. And Claire?

But that was stupid. Aisha hadn't been on the ferry, either. There were a million innocent reasons why Lucas might have stayed late on the mainland. And another million why Claire might also have stayed late.

And Lucas had come to her straight away, even sneaking up to her room. The memory warmed her. She was being dumb. She was being stupidly suspicious. Just because her parents had cheated didn't mean she should go around suspecting everyone else in the world of being unfaithful. Lucas wasn't her father, after all. And she wasn't her mother.

Lucas had come to see her, comforting her in the night, reminding her that there were still good things in the world. Those weren't the actions of a guy who had cheated on her.

Claire stole a glance across the room at Zoey. Zoey looked preoccupied, even troubled.

Well, what did you expect, Claire? she asked herself. *You wanted to lash out, and you did a swell job.* Stupid. Inexcusably stupid. What would telling Zoey about Lucas accomplish? Break the two of them up? Oh yes, that would be brilliant. Then Zoey would be free for Jake. *Yes, Claire, brilliant.*

Not to mention the fact that it was a cheap shot at Zoey, who had enough problems in her life right now. So she'd managed to be stupid and cruel at one time.

What was the matter with her? She was acting like a jealous little ninny. So Jake had gotten drunk and slept with Louise. She and Jake technically weren't boyfriend and girlfriend at that point. Technically.

Claire realized she was squeezing a pencil so hard it was in danger of snapping. With a will she relaxed her muscles.

Technically not boyfriend and girlfriend, because Jake had been busy trying to get away from Claire. She'd had to manipulate him into coming back. Manipulating was something she was good at. Unlike Zoey, who just had to look sweet and winsome and guys would fall in love. Guys didn't fall in love with Claire, at least not *that* way. Why? Was Nina right? Was Claire some sort of inhuman ice princess? Was she really ruthless and self-serving? Was that why Lucas remained fixated on Zoey, despite everything? Was that why Jake still nursed his private love for Zoey? Was that why Benjamin, who had once seemed so desperately in love with Claire, now acted like he was lucky to have escaped her?

Did Jake still love her at all, even a little? They were supposed to be going out Saturday night. Richie Felix's party. Their first real date since the ski weekend. They'd probably end up spending at least part of the evening with Zoey and Lucas. Which should be very interesting, at least.

Jake peeked from under his hand at Zoey, then shifted his gaze to Claire. Day and night. Sweet and sour. Good and evil. No, that was too strong. Claire wasn't evil. Claire was just . . . he didn't know. What was Claire exactly?

Self-contained, like she needed no one. Like the whole rest of the world could disappear tomorrow and she'd shrug it off. A perfectly beautiful creature made of stainless steel and diamonds. Indestructible, unapproachable, unstoppable.

She wasn't without feeling, she had proved that. Not without a capacity to care, because she had cared about him, perhaps still did. But her feelings and emotions were under lock and key, allowed out only when she chose to show them, turned off like a light switch whenever she wanted.

And Zoey? Zoey struck him to the heart with her vulnerability. She *was* her emotions.

Had Claire been telling the truth? Was there something between her and Lucas? It wasn't impossible, he realized sadly. And after Louise Kronenberger, he wasn't in a very good position to complain. Still, if Claire was being unfaithful, he should be very angry. He was in love with Claire, after all.

Wasn't he?

And was Claire in love with him? She'd certainly acted like she was jealous. But in love? Well, maybe something she thought was love.

But of course, Claire's only true love was Claire.

Benjamin

It isn't that the idea of my parents divorcing didn't hurt me; it did. But I guess, unlike my sister, I'm more prepared for bad things to happen. I guess the reason for that is fairly obvious—when I lost my sight it was like a bolt of lightning out of a clear blue sky, so I <u>know</u> that bad things can happen. I know it on a deep, emotional level that Zoey doesn't yet.

And maybe even before that I was more of a realist; I don't know. Maybe it's just the way I am. Not cynical, exactly, but guarded. A little bit hunkered down. Tensing up for the next beating but already telling myself it's okay, Benjamin, you'll ride through it, and thinking ha, I can take whatever the world wants to hit me with.

No, I never expected my parents to get divorced. But it didn't devastate me. The funny thing was that even during that terrible, awkward scene where they made the big announcement, I was mostly just concerned for Zoey. And oddly enough, my thoughts were less on what was happening to my family than on this new person . . . this supposed half-sister.

That probably sounds cold of me. But I'll tell you—I've done bitterness and despair. Been there, done it. It's a big damn hole that almost swallowed me up some years ago when I woke up in a hospital bed, opened my eyes, and realized that it was going to be nighttime for the rest of my life.

I don't go back to those feelings for anyone or anything. I take a wide path around them because I've learned some respect for the power of depression.

Now I focus on what I <u>can</u> do and what I still have, not what I've lost. And I think, well, it could have been worse. So in a weird way I guess I'm a sort of optimist. Just out of self-preservation.

You think about it and you realize that irrational hope is the most rational thing in the world.

Eight

That afternoon back on the island, with a sky hidden by a low, gray blanket of cloud and the empty beach and bay at their backs, Zoey and Benjamin approached a shabbily exotic Victorian building.

"This is where Christopher lives," Zoey said. "Second floor of the tower. I mean, there's a tower, on the right," she clarified. "A Sleeping Beauty kind of thing, with a pointed roof."

"Really?" Benjamin asked. "I'll have to take your word for that. You know, Dad *is* Christopher's boss, or at least one of them. It's going to be tough for Christopher to ever call in sick. Bet he's pissed."

Normally Zoey appreciated Benjamin's seemingly unfailing wit, but she was a long way from being able to see anything funny about this. "I so much don't want to do this," she said.

"Wait till Thanksgiving and Christmas," Benjamin said darkly.

"Oh, God. I hadn't even thought about that."

"Well, now that you're feeling even more upbeat, let's go on in," Benjamin suggested. "Visit Dad in his brand-new bachelor pad."

Zoey led him up onto the porch and opened the

front door. Aisha had told her not to bother knocking at this door since no one ever came down from the individual apartments to answer it. Inside was a stairway, rising up in a curve from the dusty, dim entryway.

"What do we have?" Benjamin asked. "Aside from dust and mildew; I can tell that myself."

Zoey shook her head. "It's a dump," she muttered.

"Yeah, well, let's not tell Dad that. Besides, how bad is it, actually?"

"Like something from an old black-and-white detective movie."

"Cool," Benjamin said impishly. "Maybe Dad can become a hard-boiled private eye."

"Not really very cool," Zoey said tersely. "I guess he's upstairs. Here, that's the railing."

"Hmm. A substantial banister." He ran his hand along the smooth wood. "I love a substantial banister."

Zoey was tired of trying to be nice. "Benjamin, if you're acting this way because you think I need to be cheered up, forget it."

"I didn't realize I was bothering you." He started up the stairs cautiously, the way he always had to be in unexplored territory. "A left curve beginning at the fourth step, one, two, three, four, and we straighten out again. Am I still annoying you?" he asked playfully.

"I just don't see much humor in this."

"There's humor in everything, Zoey, or just about everything. Seventeen steps and we're up. Must have nice high ceilings in the building."

"Okay, we're in a hallway, maybe four different doors," Zoey explained.

"Left," Benjamin said confidently.

"How do you know?"

"Listen," he urged. "Lyle Lovett. *If I were the man you wanted*. Playing on a portable CD player. I think the old man raided my CDs."

Zoey looked at him sharply. Was this some kind of a joke? But no, Benjamin looked much more serious now, even a little sad. And when she concentrated, she heard the music.

"Jeez, Zoey," Benjamin said under his breath. "Kind of a depressing song to be listening to." He let out a sigh. "I'd feel so much better about this if he was listening to . . . I don't know, like one of his old Stones albums. Something tougher. Divorce and country music. Man."

Zoey led the way down the hall, following the music, which grew loud as they reached the door. She took a deep, steadying breath and tried out a cheerful smile that wasn't going to last two minutes. She knocked.

"Let's just hope he doesn't have a woman in there," Benjamin said, reverting to black humor.

The door opened. Their father's face was eager, hopeful, for just a second before he recognized them and his expression crashed. Zoey realized he'd been hoping the knock was his wife, not his kids. He made an attempt to revive, trying his best to work up a devil-may-care look, but in the end he turned away quickly, hiding the pain that he couldn't keep from his face.

"Hi, Daddy," Zoey said. She pursued him, caught up, and managed to plant a clumsy kiss on his cheek.

"Hey," Mr. Passmore said, his ragged voice loaded with desperately fake cheer. "I didn't expect visitors so soon." He waved a hand around the room. "I haven't exactly got the place decorated just yet."

He was wearing a sweater Ms. Passmore had given him for his birthday. Zoey took in the room, trying not to linger too long on the opened suitcase full of rumpled clothing, the sagging bed, the dirty window opening onto the beach, a view that instead of making the room more attractive just seemed to add to the seedy sense of decay.

"Pretty grim, huh?" Mr. Passmore said with a self-deprecating look.

"It could use some flowers or something," Zoey said.

"Yeah." He nodded, as if this was a profoundly important suggestion. "Your mom always says that. You know, flowers . . . and, you know." He looked around again, unwilling to meet Zoey's eyes. "I guess some over there." He pointed to the low counter that separated the minuscule kitchen from the rest of the single room. "Some of those, what are those white flowers? You know, all the little petals and everything."

"Chrysanthemums," Benjamin said, surprising Zoey. "I remember them," he explained. "Roses and chrysanthemums."

"Flowers," their father said, nodding.

Silence descended, and Lyle's sad lyrics still swelled clear, speaking of lost loves and futility.

Zoey fought the urge to turn off the offending music.

"I'm guessing this song was written *before* he got with Julia Roberts," Benjamin said dryly.

"I suppose it is kind of depressing," Mr. Passmore said. He stared blankly at the CD player.

"It's a depressing situation," Benjamin said.

"Sorry."

Zoey was on the verge of telling him it wasn't his fault, a sort of automatic urge to offer comfort. But of course it was his fault, almost as much as her mother's. "Maybe things will still work out," Zoey said.

Her father's eyes were filled with tears. "Yeah," he said, sounding strangled.

Zoey saw Benjamin clench his fist involuntarily. His mouth was a tight line as he struggled to control his own emotions. Benjamin couldn't see the tears, Zoey realized, but he had heard them in that single desperate word.

"Well, we just wanted to see where you were," Zoey said.

"I'm right here."

"God, Daddy, what am I supposed to say? I hate this!" Zoey cried. "You shouldn't be ... here ... you should ..." Sobs had broken up her rush of pointless, meaningless words.

Her father opened his arms and took her to him. She cried, spilling her tears on his shoulder. And then she felt her father reach out and take Benjamin into the same embrace.

Claire took a slow walk around the circumference of her widow's walk, feeling agitated, even emotional. A storm, that's what she needed. A major, serious, blow the damned lights out, drown the streets, knock the branches off the trees storm. That would clear her mind.

But all she saw as she looked around from her high, private perch was gray cloud, lying so low it was like she could reach up over her head and touch it. It spread from far beyond Weymouth, still sparkling with car headlights and traffic signals, across the bay, over the island, far out beyond the range of sight above the Atlantic.

North Harbor was settling into darkness. Darkness had already crept under the sparse shrubs, down the narrow alleys, up the eastern walls. The sea had gone from gray-green to the color of molten lead, and to the east the sky was already black. The green warning light at the end of the breakwater was on. The sweeping beacon from the lighthouse would be coming on shortly, warning boats away from the island's northern point.

Normally Claire would have found something of interest even in this tiresomely consistent weather pattern. The idea that the sun was still up there, shining brightly above the clouds far to the west, and that away to the east the tops of those clouds were silver with moonlight . . . that usually would have held a certain poetry for her.

But this evening peace was hard to find. She was feeling foul and dangerous. Angry, with no real target in sight aside from herself. Was it just that Nina's happiness was getting on her nerves? That would have been way too petty. Was it that whole stupid episode on the stairs with Zoey and Jake?

Yes, that was part of it. She'd blown up in an attack of pure, spiteful jealousy. Pitiful. Tonight he was away with the football team, playing a road game in Lewiston. But tomorrow night they were going to that stupid party. How was she supposed to act? Should she just abandon the last of her pride and ask him outright, Jake, do you love me? Do you care at all, really, deep down?

She shook her head violently, throwing off the feeling, but not losing the underlying sense of anger.

She took a last, unsatisfied look around and descended through the hatchway, climbing the ladder easily from long practice.

She checked the little weather station she kept. Barometer unchanged. No wind to speak of. Temperature thirty-seven degrees.

She flopped down at her desk and turned on her computer, typing in the code that took her to the America Online software. She'd purchased the software to use its weather features and for the access to certain research. Living on the island made casual runs to the library difficult.

She pressed F-10 to pull down the bar menu, and she went to the weather maps. Slowly a map formed on her screen, a map that showed unbroken gray cloud cover from a hundred miles out in the Atlantic, extending inland over all of New England.

"I could really use a storm," Claire told the screen.

She bailed out of the weather maps and was on the verge of leaving the program altogether. But her eye was drawn to the pull-down menu line for CB, the talk lines. She had homework to do, but she was too distracted for study. Nina would already have occupied the TV and seized the remote control.

Claire chose the general band, and a prompt appeared asking her to pick a handle.

"A name," she muttered. She considered for a moment before typing in W-e-a-t-h-e-r G-i-r-l.

A grid came on screen, a series of channels. She scanned forward and stopped at one labeled 17-TEEN ONLY.

Enter.

The screen went black and divided into two parts: a large upper screen and a much smaller box below labeled INPUT. Instantly the upper screen began scrolling.

————[17] TEEN ONLY————

Babyface	i dint say you were a jerk
!MoFo!	anyone here like the Breeters? Breeders.
Babyface	i was saying you sounded like a jerk
COBAIN	i feel stupid and contagious
<DooMeeeNow>	babyface if i sound like a jerk i must be a jerkand that's why
Bad2daBone	your half right, Cobain. hehe hehe.
<DooMeeeNow>	i'm pissed off at you, babyface
(:Z!ppy:)	Hi.
!MoFo!	Lol, Bad2.
COBAIN	chew me, Bad2. you too mofo.
(:Z!ppy:)	hey what's lol mean? im new here.
Babyface	peace, DooMeee. chill, okay. take a prozac.
!MoFo!	lol=laughing out loud
Babyface	take 2 prozac.

It took Claire a few minutes to begin to get the basics of what was happening. It was like trying to listen to half a dozen different conversations at once. And none of them was exactly interesting.

————[17] TEEN ONLY————

++Vedder++	Hey cobain step off man or i'll kick yer a$$.
Flyer	Hi. the usual brilliant conversation, I see. using

COBAIN	Vedder you wuss
Flyer	the information superhighway to its fullest potential.
!MoFo!	age and sex check!
<DooMeeeNow>	are there any girls here? any horny females?
Flyer	Gee, DooMeee, with that handle and such a subtle come-on I'm sure there are
COBAIN	16, male
Flyer	several females who'd be interested in you. not HUMAN females maybe . . .
++Vedder++	17, more male than Cobain
Babyface	15, girl
<DooMeeeNow>	studly 16
!MoFo!	14, dude
Flyer	17, male. now can we not have another age check for at least five minutes?

Suddenly there was a beep and a smaller box, superimposed and divided in half horizontally, appeared. It showed the name FLYER at the top.

---
[1] Flyer

How about you, Weather Girl? Not talking?

Claire was alarmed. How did Flyer know she was there watching? She hadn't said anything. She tabbed to the input box and typed "How do you know I'm here?" Enter.

The answer came quickly. There was a way to use the pull-down menu to find out who was monitoring

the conversation. He was interested in her handle.
"Why Weather Girl?"

Well, Claire decided, this was idiotic. Now she
felt trapped in a conversation with some guy whose
name she didn't know, whom she could not see,
who, for all she knew, might live three thousand
miles away.

Nevertheless, she typed in "I'm interested in
weather."

"Why?"

"Because" . . . Why was she explaining herself?
On the other hand, why not. People almost never
asked her *why* she enjoyed weather. They usually
just nodded, figured she was eccentric, and went on
to the next topic. "Because it has such power to
affect us and remains something we can't control.
Because it's this huge system, all interconnected so
that katabatic winds in Antarctica, and warm spots
in the Pacific, and evaporation off the Caspian Sea
all work together in incredible complexity."

"Oh, my God. Someone on CB with an actual
brain," Flyer said. "It's almost a miracle. Complete
sentences. Punctuation, even."

"Thanks. I guess."

"No, thank you. I've spent a lot of my dad's
money scanning CB for someone with half a brain,
and I found someone with a whole one."

"You do this a lot?" Claire asked.

Suddenly a second box appeared. This time the
caller was named Long Johnson. "Hey, weathergirl.
tell me what you have on."

Claire stared at this for a moment, then hit the
escape button and returned to Flyer.

"Hey, Flyer. Some guy just popped up and asked
me what I have on. What's that about?"

"Perv," Flyer wrote back. "We get them sometimes. Just ignore the guy; he'll go away. Answering previous question, yes, I do this fairly often."

Claire considered that for a moment, along with the creep who'd asked her what she was wearing. It was very likely that the people on the system were techno-nerds and creeps. On the other hand, *she* was on the system.

"Where are you, Flyer?"

"I'm in Manchester, NH, charm city. Your profile shows you're using an access number in Portland."

Close enough, Claire decided. She wasn't going to give away any more than that.

"Damn," Flyer typed back, "I have to go now. My mom is yelling something about dinner. But please, please come back on tomorrow. I'll wait for you."

"Why?"

"Because you sound interesting, Weather Girl."

"By the way, why the name 'Flyer'?"

"I'm getting my pilot's license. Have to go, but come again tomorrow, okay?"

"If I have time."

"Bye, Weather Girl."

"Bye, Flyer."

The box disappeared. She was back to the main screen, where COBAIN and !MoFo! were now insulting each other. She bailed out and turned off the computer.

Odd. Very odd. She doubted she would do it again.

Nine

The kitchen was empty, Benjamin was sure of that. He listened closely to the sounds of the house, wanting to make sure no one else was within range to overhear what he was doing. From upstairs he heard a creak; Zoey in her room. From the living room, the faint sounds of the television. His mother.

He paused to consider. His mother might get up at any moment and come to the kitchen for something to eat or drink. And that would be a little embarrassing.

Oh, well. It was either take his chances with the kitchen phone or be overheard using the upstairs hall phone.

He sat down at the table, placed a pad of paper and a ballpoint pen in front of him, and lifted the receiver. He dialed information.

"Yes, do you have listings for Kittery? The McAvoy residence. Sorry, I don't have a first name." He sighed. "Okay, better give me all six, then."

He grabbed the pen and, using the hard tip, began pressing dots into the paper, a sort of Braille shorthand. He had an excellent memory for numbers, but even he couldn't recall six phone numbers. He hung up the phone, tore off the sheet, and turned the paper over. Now he could read off the dots with his fingertips. He dialed.

"Yes, is this the McAvoy residence? Oh, hi. Look, my name is . . . um, Jack. I'm a friend of your daughter Lara . . . You don't have a daughter? Gee, sorry, I must have the wrong number."

He went on to the next number and got an answering machine. He didn't leave a message. On the fifth call he got lucky. This McAvoy residence *did* have a daughter, and yes, she was named Lara.

"Well, ma'am, I'm an old friend of hers and I was just wondering if she was there this evening?"

No, she wasn't. Where had he known her?

"It's been a long time," Benjamin said smoothly. "I knew her in junior high."

Why was he calling her up now, after all this time?

Hmmm. Excellent question. "To tell you the truth, I know it's silly, but in eighth grade I borrowed a book from her and I just came across it in some old boxes and I wanted to return it."

He was rather pleased with himself for having come up with that on the spur of the moment.

But mom—he assumed it was Lara's mother he was speaking to—didn't see why Lara would care about an old book. It occurred to Benjamin only then that this woman on the other end of the line had once been his father's secret lover in Europe. Where in Europe, he wondered vaguely. Paris, maybe, or Venice.

"Yes, I know, but I can't keep something that doesn't belong to me," he argued. "It just isn't right."

Mom McAvoy couldn't exactly argue with that. If he'd leave his number, she'd pass it along to Lara. She might be down next weekend.

"Down?" Benjamin pursued hopefully.

Yes, down from Weymouth.

"She lives in Weymouth now?" Benjamin said.

That wasn't really any of his business, but if he wanted to leave a number . . .

Benjamin gave her the first number that came to mind, which happened to be that of a used-car dealer whose annoying TV ads had drilled the number into his brain, and spelled out his name J-a-c-k B-a-t-e-s.

He hung up. So. Lara McAvoy, the mysterious half-sister, lived in Weymouth. How convenient. He dialed information again. "In Weymouth, please, the number for Lara McAvoy, or initial L McAvoy."

Just one number this time, under L. McAvoy. He took a deep breath and let it out slowly. He dialed. Four rings before the phone was picked up. A brusque male voice.

He pitched his own voice as low as it would go. "Uh, yeah, is this the Lara McAvoy residence?"

Yeah, she lived there, so what?

"This is UPS; we have a package for her, but the address label is torn. Looks like Third Street, or it could be Blakely; not our fault since the label is improperly attached."

It wasn't either of those addresses, the voice said. Not even close.

Benjamin held his breath.

The voice gave him the correct address and hung up the phone.

Benjamin settled the receiver.

729 Independence, apartment 402. Amazing. He

practically walked past it on his way from the ferry landing to school every day. All the time, his half-sister right there, unknown to him. Wasn't life full of little surprises?

If only he could see her, this half-sister. If only he could see her face, and find the similarities between her face and his own. There should be some similarity if they shared the same father.

People had always told Benjamin that he'd gotten his mother's good looks—her cheekbones, her eyes. No one had ever said he looked like his father. He had an uncle, his father's brother, who used to joke about it, saying how lucky he was to look like his beautiful mother and not like his scruffy dad, ha ha ha. And he'd never thought anything of it before. But now he had done the math and whatever his mother said or believed, it was possible that his father wasn't his father at all.

If his father was indeed his father, then a keen eye should be able to find some similarity between Benjamin and this Lara. He crumpled up his Braille notepad, counted the steps to the trash can, and dropped it in.

Late Friday night, and Aisha was finding it a little difficult walking down Climbing Way wearing shoes with heels, and a little cold walking through the night with her legs bare below the hem of her dress. Stockings didn't exactly keep out the October wind. But she'd asked Christopher if she should dress up and he'd said sure, why not? She'd taken it almost as a challenge and had gone all out.

She'd sort of overlooked the fact that with the death of the family's island car, she would have to walk down to the restaurant dressed like she was on her way to dinner at the White House, her leather jacket doing nothing at all to keep her legs and toes warm. Then, as she passed through downtown, she'd encountered the problem of heels on cobblestones.

She was cold but still excited when she arrived at the door of the restaurant. The sign on the door said CLOSED, but she went inside, grateful for the warmth. She took off her jacket and hung it on a peg. The restaurant was empty. A single candle burned on one corner table, flickering from the crystal, casting shadows on the white linen tablecloth. The only other light was the cheerful golden glow from the fireplace. She fluffed her hair and straightened her outfit.

"Christopher?" No answer. Louder, "Christopher?"

The swinging door to the kitchen opened, revealing a rectangle of brilliant fluorescence, then closed again. Christopher appeared, looking like he, too, was on his way to the White House for dinner.

"Hi," he said.

"Hi, back."

"You look beautiful," he said.

"You look okay, too."

He came closer, then stopped. "If I come any closer," he said, "you'll look just way too good."

"I'll take my chances," she said.

He took her in his arms and they kissed. He was the first to pull away. "Hey, I'm not just your little love toy," he said playfully. "I have an evening planned here."

"Oh, really?"

"This way, please." He led her to the small, candlelit table and pulled her chair out for her. She sat down and he yanked the napkin neatly from the table, unfolded it, and laid it in her lap.

"You didn't eat much for dinner, did you?" he asked suspiciously.

"You told me not to. I'm starving."

"Excellent."

"Where's *your* chair?" she asked.

He shook his head. "No, tonight I wait on you alone." He reached behind her and she heard the slushy sound of ice. He produced a bottle and showed it to her. "Moët & Chandon Brut. Unfortunately, we don't carry Dom Perignon. Or maybe it's fortunate, since DP costs a hundred and twenty a bottle in most restaurants."

"Champagne?"

"Of course, champagne. No one's driving tonight," he said with a conspiratorial wink. He unfastened the cage, wrapped a clean napkin around the neck, and twisted the cork neatly, a muted pop.

Aisha looked around a little nervously.

"Don't worry, miss," Christopher said, pouring her a glass of the wine. "I told Mr. Passmore what I was up to. He went for it. He's very susceptible to anything romantic right now, poor guy. I guess you know about the whole divorce thing."

"Yes," Aisha said. "I really—"

"Hush," Christopher held up a hand. "Nothing sad or depressing tonight."

"Absolutely," Aisha agreed. She took a sip of the champagne. "Excellent. The finest champagne I've ever tasted. Of course, the only other champagne I've ever had was at my aunt's wedding."

"Good. Then I'll bring on the first course."

"Aren't you going to have some?"

"I am your servant tonight," he said.

"You mean you'll do anything I want?"

"Yes. Anything."

"Mmmm. That certainly gives me something to think about," Aisha said. "Kind of a change in attitude for you, isn't it?" She asked the question playfully, but his answer was utterly serious.

"Yes, it is," he said. "I got kind of a second chance at a life yesterday. I decided in this life I'd be a nicer person."

"You were always a nice person," Aisha said with feeling.

"Not always to you, though," Christopher said. "As of tonight that's changed."

"And now you'll do whatever I want?"

"Well, for tonight, anyway," he said.

"Then you'd better kiss me," Aisha said.

He leaned down and kissed her for a very long time, a time that banished every memory of cold and left Aisha wondering whether the all-body tingle she was feeling came from the tiny sip of champagne.

He straightened up.

"Don't go," she breathed.

"Hey, I have a risotto going in the kitchen," he said. "Even for you I don't ruin a risotto."

"Risotto? You mean like that Rice-a-Roni stuff?"

His look was one of pure horror. "Aisha, because I love you I'm going to forget you said that."

"Um, would you say that again?" Aisha said.

He looked puzzled. "You mean 'risotto'?"

"You know what I mean."

He came back to her. And then he knelt beside her, bringing his face level with her own. "You mean, 'I love you'?"

"Yes. That was it."

"I do love you, Eesh. I was slow to figure it out, but now that I have, I promise never to forget it."

Nina lay in her bed and talked to Benjamin on the phone for half an hour. While she talked, she drew in her sketchbook. After they had talked for half an hour, it took fifteen more minutes to say good night. Benjamin had sounded distracted but not depressed. Distracted was good in Benjamin—he liked to have things to think about. After she hung up the phone, Nina lay awake in bed with the lights out for a while, playing a CD he had loaned her. It was baroque guitar, not exactly her usual thing, but Benjamin liked it and she wanted to understand everything about him. When she finally turned it off, she had to resist a powerful urge to call him back. Instead she told the darkness again that she loved him and went to sleep.

Claire lay against her mountain of carefully arranged pillows and read a book called *The Last Wilderness*. It was about Antarctica. It was Claire's goal to go to Antarctica when she'd finished college. It was the greatest place on earth to study weather at its most severe. The first year she'd stay just for the austral summer, maybe at Palmer base or McMurdo. Then, with more experience, she'd get to winter over. As far from civilization as a human being could get. As cold, hostile, and alien an environment as could be found. She had turned a dozen pages of the book before she realized she hadn't retained any of what she'd read. Her mind wasn't on Antarctica. It was on Jake, not far but very near. Simple, straightforward, never subtle, not even especially intelligent Jake. Almost a dumb jock, really. Not especially handsome to her eye, or particularly sexy. Just a dumb jock she wished loved her.

Aisha tried to sleep but couldn't, not even after the big meal and the champagne. The meal had been followed by what seemed like hours of long, slow, lingering kisses that had left her buzzing and giddy. Christopher said he had changed, but fortunately there were some things about him that hadn't changed at all, and the memory of those things kept her in a drifting, half-sleeping, half-waking state, smiling into the dark, sighing into her pillow. It was really Aisha who had changed, she realized. What had happened to the girl who dismissed moony-eyed romanticism as juvenile? What had happened to Aisha-like-a-rock, the girl who couldn't be distracted by mere guys from the more important issues of life? She seemed to have completely forgotten what those more important issues might be. The important issue now was that in a few hours Christopher would come by on his rounds and she would get to see him again.

Zoey fell straight asleep, exhausted. She woke after an hour and lay staring up at the ceiling. She'd had a dream. She didn't remember the details, but it had left her feeling sad and defenseless against her emotions. She wanted her old life back. She wanted her father and mother together in the next room. She wanted to erase what she had heard and learned, and especially what she had seen. She wanted to forget her mother screaming hysterical accusations at her bedroom door. She wanted to forget the image of her father in his apartment, looking like he'd had his heart torn out. She wanted to go back to being the girl who smiled more and laughed more and feared for nothing. The girl who collected quotes and wrote her endless first chapter of her never-to-be-finished romance novel. And, as incongruous as it was to feel this way, she wanted to wake up like she had that morning, with her head resting on Lucas's chest, to hear his heart beating and feel his arm around her.

Zoey

I read a quote by Oscar
Wilde. I used to collect
quotes and post them over
my desk in the dormer be-
cause I thought that way I
would learn to be wise and
understanding. But this
quote just shows what a
silly idea that is.

Oscar Wilde said <u>Chil-
dren begin by loving their
parents: after a time they
judge them; rarely, if ever,
do they forgive them.</u>

It was so right on target
with what has been going
on in my own life. I had
loved my parents. Then I
had judged them. Now I
have no desire to forgive
them. But the problem is
that Wilde was being hu-
morous. He was a sarcastic,
ironic man who said many
very clever things that

were designed to make people laugh and say oh, that
Oscar, he's so witty.

For him it was a laugh;
for me it's just the truth.
Nothing funny about it. I
will never forgive my parents, especially my mother,
for what they did. I know
I'm supposed to be all
mature and reasonable and
understand that they are
just people, after all. Just
people who occasionally
screw up. But they aren't
just people. They're my
parents. Wait, forget that.
Just say that they are parents, period. That means
they have to deal with being
parents. And that means
they have to make sure their
kids have a family. And if
that gets in the way of what
they want, too bad.

My mom told me I might be

sorry one day for the way
I had judged her. But no,
I don't think so. See, I'm
living with the results.
I'm the one whose family
is screwed up. I'm the one
who had to go visit her father in his pathetic little
apartment. Why should I
forgive?

I will get on with my life,
I've decided that. I will do
the best I can not to let
this mess me up, but forget
about forgiveness.

Ten

Zoey called Aisha at nine forty-five on Saturday morning and announced that she had a shopping mission to perform. By ten forty-five the two of them were dressed and pounding on the door of the Geiger home. Claire answered, looked them over, and refused their invitation. They found Nina in her room, drawing on a sketch pad, headphones blasting Nirvana so that she hadn't heard their knocking. In a small, distracted voice she was singing *Hey. Wait. I've got a new complaint.*

Zoey and Aisha crept in and without warning jumped on her bed. Nina tore the earphones from her head.

"You two are going to give me a heart attack!" Nina yelled. "I could have peed on myself."

Aisha grabbed the sketch pad and whistled. Nina jumped up, looking horrified, and yanked the pad away again. "Hey, you can't look at that."

"What was it?" Zoey asked Aisha.

Aisha batted her lashes coyly. "It looked like a drawing of someone we all know."

"Hmm. A *male* someone?" Zoey asked, wonderfully entertained by the way Nina was blushing.

"A cute male someone," Aisha confirmed. "*With* sunglasses, but *without* shirt. Also, small heart in the corner with the names Nina and Benjamin in it. Very junior high, although the drawing was pretty good."

Zoey smiled at Nina. "Where is the tough, unsentimental girl we all once knew?"

"I'm trying to develop my skill as an artist," Nina argued unconvincingly.

"And you just thought you'd start with boy nipples as a subject," Aisha teased. "When have you seen Benjamin without his shirt on, anyway! Seems kind of suspicious to me."

"When we all go swimming down at Big Bite," Nina said, now several shades redder than usual.

"And in your dreams, when you wake up going unh, unh, oh Benjamin, more, more, oh yes, Benjamin, oh yes, yes—" A pillow swung with some force interrupted Aisha's rendition. "Hey!"

"Don't make me use this again," Nina warned, holding the pillow like a weapon.

"It's okay," Aisha said. "I know love makes people do strange things. Like hitting people with pillows." She gave Nina a dirty look.

"Is there a reason why you two came by to torture me?" Nina demanded.

"I have a shopping mission," Zoey said solemnly.

"A shopping mission?" Nina echoed.

Zoey reached into her bag and pulled out a piece of paper. "Exhibit A: the list." She dug into her wallet and held up a credit card. "Exhibit B: my dad's MasterCard."

"Excellent," Nina said. "The mall zone?"

"We will crawl the mall," Aisha said.

"We will empty the mall," Zoey said. "By the

time we're done, there will be no mall."

"What's the mission, anyway?" Nina asked as she shucked off her rumpled clothes and scrounged for new rumpled clothes on the floor of her closet.

"I went over to my dad's apartment again this morning, early. It's kind of not-very-decorated or set up, so we made out a list of stuff he needed."

Nina exchanged a look with Aisha. "That must have been kind of—what's the word?" Nina said.

"Awkward?" Aisha suggested. "Strange?"

"Yeah, at least," Nina said. She found a sweater and slipped it on over her head. When her head poked through she added, "Didn't it bother you a little?"

It had bothered her terribly, Zoey admitted to herself. She shrugged. "I'm trying to adjust, you know? It's pretty bad and all, but still, he needs towels and a scritchy thing for pots and pans and some curtains."

Aisha shook her head sadly and gave Zoey a doleful look.

"Stop it, you guys," Zoey said impatiently. "I'm trying to act like this is all perfectly normal."

Aisha shook her head again. "If my parents ever broke up, I'd feel like killing myself. Wait a minute," she added in alarm. "I didn't mean that. I mean, don't kill yourself or anything."

Zoey smiled. "Good thing you added that last part, Eesh, or I might have just run out and hanged myself."

"I guess you don't want to talk about it, huh?" Aisha said.

"What is there to talk about? People get divorced all the time. Look at all the kids at school whose parents are divorced."

"Easier to count the ones who *aren't*," Nina agreed. "Still, you know, I guess it's not something you think will happen to your own parents."

"No," Zoey said, staring blankly at Nina's desk.

Nina sounded uncomfortable and made a show of paying attention to her hair in the mirror. "I mean, when my mom died it was like that. You always think that kind of thing happens to other people."

Zoey heard the quiver in Nina's voice, and it unleashed the emotions she'd worked so hard at suppressing all morning. "Damn. Here goes my makeup." She brushed away a tear.

Nina sat beside her on the bed and put her arm around her. "I know it doesn't help, but I'm really sorry this had to happen."

The tears came freely now and she realized that both her friends had their arms around her, and both of them were crying as well.

"God, Nina, your mom dies, my parents get divorced . . ." Zoey shook her head.

Aisha drew away. "I almost feel guilty," she said.

Zoey made a blubbering laugh. "It's okay, Aisha."

"Yeah, you're probably next," Nina said.

Zoey and Nina both began giggling through their tears. Aisha didn't find it nearly as funny, which just made Zoey laugh all the harder.

There was a knock on the door and Mr. Geiger stuck his head in. "Say, Nina, if you're going over . . . to . . . the . . . mainland—" He fell silent and stared uncertainly at the spectacle of three girls, tears streaming down their cheeks, taking turns giggling hysterically and sobbing pitifully. "Never mind." He closed the door quickly.

*   *   *

Lucas lay flat on his surfboard, riding the annoyingly gentle swell, waiting for one more half-decent wave and wondering whether his feet were frostbitten. He was just going to have to move to California or Hawaii someday. East Coast surf was never that great, and here in Maine it was almost impossible. He'd gotten about four decent waves in the two hours he'd been freezing out here. Four decent waves and the fifth had been a long time in coming, but if he wasn't mistaken, it was rolling in right now.

He turned toward the shore, judged the timing, and began paddling to match speed with the wave. The leading edge of the surge caught him and he was up, nimbly pulling his numb feet under him, standing, wobbling, fighting to stay up.

An outcropping of bleached granite was just ahead, marked by explosions of water. This was the fun part. He shifted his weight and cut right, against the grain, coming as close to the rock as he could, flying past, but so near he could almost have reached out and touched it.

The wave broke on the gravel shore and Lucas rolled off the board into the surf. He came up laughing happily and saw a figure standing on the beach, shaking his head in derisive amusement.

"The things you white boys will do for fun," Christopher said.

"You should try it sometime," Lucas said. He squeezed water back out of his hair.

"Pretty weak waves, aren't they? Not exactly like they are on *Baywatch*."

Lucas nodded. "Yeah, but see, I add the extra element of playing tag with the rocks. I could easily have had my brains bashed out."

"Then it all makes sense," Christopher agreed. "You up for something?"

"What?" Lucas began peeling off his wet suit and putting on his warm, dry clothes.

"There's a car I'm thinking of buying. I thought maybe since I know zip about cars you'd come look it over with me."

"A real car or an island car?"

"Island car. I just need it for delivering my papers in the morning. It's getting slightly cold for the bike. Plus I can use a car to make pick-ups for people at the ferry."

Lucas grinned. "Also, it's hard to use the backseat of a bike for making out."

"You forget, *I* have my own apartment."

"*You* forget—Aisha walked in on you there when you had that other girl with you." He finished dressing and bundled his wet suit into a zipper bag.

"That's not going to be a problem in the future," Christopher said.

Lucas looked at him more closely. He'd seen that look before. On himself, for one. "So you and Aisha are all straightened out now?"

Christopher's grin was part smugness, part dreaminess, part memory. "Mmmm, definitely." He sighed, grinned wider, then sighed again. "We've decided just to make it a thing between us only. I mean, you know, just see each other."

"Christopher, you're too much of a dog to be serious."

"Things change," Christopher said.

"Sometimes for the better, sometimes for the worse," Lucas said. He tossed Christopher his bag. "I'll carry the board." They started across the beach, climbing up to the road.

"Yeah, we're practically an old, boring, stable couple now, like you and Zoey," Christopher teased.

"Well, I don't know how stable Zoey and I are," Lucas said. Surfing, even bad surfing on an indifferent ocean, always drove every other concern out of his mind. He'd started years earlier, when it had been an escape from his father, and in a way from his own confused, angry mind. Now it was like he was walking back into reality.

"Maybe you should back off a little," Christopher suggested. "You know, you keep pushing Zoey, she'll just get more stubborn."

Lucas laughed. "Says the voice of experience. It's not about that. It's not about sex."

"It's not?"

"This part of it isn't about sex," Lucas clarified. "Okay, it's about sex in a way, but it's not because I've been trying to pressure her or anything. It's more about . . . something else."

Christopher leered. *"Who's* the something else?"

Lucas looked around guiltily. "You can't tell Aisha, all right?"

Christopher stopped. They had reached the edge of town, and Lucas leaned his board against a tall wood fence. "Tell Dr. Shupe," Christopher said. "Just because I can't be a hound anymore doesn't mean I go around telling male secrets to members of the opposite sex."

"See, I was pissed at Zoey because of, you know—"

"Oh, yeah, I know." He wiggled his eyebrows suggestively.

"I was also pissed because I saw her hugging Jake. Which Claire also saw. But neither of us, me or Claire I mean, neither of us knew about this whole thing with Zoey's mom and Jake's dad and all this divorce crap, so we were just pissed off because it looked like Zoey and Jake were . . ." Lucas trailed off and took a deep breath. He scrabbled his wet hair violently with both hands. He focused on a rough patch on the wax coating of his surfboard.

"Don't go stupid on me," Christopher said impatiently.

"Look, I was mad at Zoey, Claire was mad at Jake, we ended up going for a drive . . ." He picked at the patch of peeling wax.

"You and *Claire?*" Christopher's jaw actually dropped open. "You and Claire? Wow. Huh. So, what did you do?"

Lucas waved a hand dismissively. "Made out a little."

"Kissing?"

"Uh-huh."

"Tongue?"

Lucas nodded.

"Were any buttons or zippers involved?"

Lucas shrugged noncommittally.

"Little tiny snaps?"

"We didn't like do *it* or anything," Lucas said, putting an end to the inquiry.

"Does Zoey know?"

"Yeah," Lucas said sarcastically, "I went straight to her house and told her the whole thing in complete detail."

Christopher looked at him with a mixture of envy and pity.

"You are so screwed, boy, if she ever finds out."

"I thought maybe I *should* tell her. I mean, you

know, get it all out there. I think she'll let it go,"
he added, sounding unconvincing even to himself.

Christopher sneered. "Yeah, right. You must have
gotten salt water in your brain, man. Check it out—
her parents are getting divorced because her father
was screwing around like twenty years ago, right?
And her mother was doing payback with Mr.
McRoyan. Now along comes Lucas. Lucas *thinks*
Zoey was screwing around with Jake, so Lucas tries
a little payback with Claire. You see any problem
there, Lucas?"

"It's not *exactly* the same," Lucas said weakly.

"Very, very close, dude. If you think Zoey is going to be all forgiving about you and Claire Geiger
in the backseat of her daddy's Mercedes . . . man,
you are dumb."

---

[1] Flyer

You came back.

---

[2] Weather Girl

I didn't have anything else to do. Nothing on TV on
Saturday afternoon.

---

[1] Flyer

I'm glad you came. I soloed this morning. Meaning I
took my first flight without an instructor.

---

[2] Weather Girl

Congratulations. Weren't you nervous?

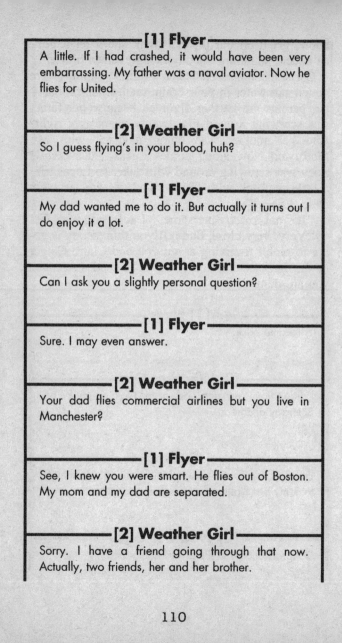

[1] Flyer

A little. If I had crashed, it would have been very embarrassing. My father was a naval aviator. Now he flies for United.

[2] Weather Girl

So I guess flying's in your blood, huh?

[1] Flyer

My dad wanted me to do it. But actually it turns out I do enjoy it a lot.

[2] Weather Girl

Can I ask you a slightly personal question?

[1] Flyer

Sure. I may even answer.

[2] Weather Girl

Your dad flies commercial airlines but you live in Manchester?

[1] Flyer

See, I knew you were smart. He flies out of Boston. My mom and my dad are separated.

[2] Weather Girl

Sorry. I have a friend going through that now. Actually, two friends, her and her brother.

━━[1] Flyer━━

Tell them it does get to seem more normal after a while. Not like it's no big deal, exactly, but it does get more normal, having your mother in one place, your father somewhere else. How are they doing, your friends?

━━[2] Weather Girl━━

I don't really know.

━━[1] Flyer━━

You mean they don't want to talk about it?

━━[1] Flyer━━

Are you still there, WG?

━━[2] Weather Girl━━

I'm here.

━━[1] Flyer━━

Is something the matter?

━━[2] Weather Girl━━

No. I was just thinking.

━━[1] Flyer━━

What were you thinking?

[2] Weather Girl

I don't know how my friends feel about this divorce because I don't know how they feel about anything. I didn't ask. And I'm not exactly the person everyone comes to with their problems. I don't know why I should be telling you this.

[1] Flyer

Because I'm just a line of type on a computer screen, WG. I'm a safe person to talk to.

[2] Weather Girl

I guess that's it.

[1] Flyer

So, not very popular, huh?

[2] Weather Girl

Actually, I guess I am popular in some ways. It's just not something I care about. I mean, I have friends; they just don't open up to me very much.

[1] Flyer

Do they think you'll disapprove?

[2] Weather Girl

No. I guess they just don't think I'm very sympathetic. Or maybe they think I'll use things they tell me for my own advantage.

[1] Flyer
You're very complicated, aren't you?

[2] Weather Girl
You could say that.

[1] Flyer
I like complicated.

[2] Weather Girl
Thanks. I have to go now.

[1] Flyer
You have to?

[2] Weather Girl
Have to get ready for tonight.

[1] Flyer
Oh. Major date?

[2] Weather Girl
A date. I don't know how major.

[1] Flyer
Just my luck; you have a boyfriend.

[2] Weather Girl

For now. We'll see.

[1] Flyer

That sounds interesting, but I guess we'll talk about that another day. By the way, my name is Sean.

[1] Flyer

Still there, or did you already sign off?

[2] Weather Girl

I was deciding whether I should give you my name. But I realized you wouldn't even know if it was my real name. So: it's Claire.

[1] Flyer

Claire. Perfect. It's exactly right.

[2] Weather Girl

Maybe that's not my real name.

[1] Flyer

No, I think it is.

[2] Weather Girl

Why?

━━━ [1] Flyer ━━━

Because I think you want to be sincere with me.

━━━ [2] Weather Girl ━━━

Sincerity is not the first thing people who know me think of when they hear my name mentioned.

━━━ [1] Flyer ━━━

All the more reason for you to want to be sincere with me.

━━━ [2] Weather Girl ━━━

I like the name Sean.

━━━ [1] Flyer ━━━

I like the name Claire. Even if it isn't your real name.

━━━ [2] Weather Girl ━━━

I have to go.

━━━ [1] Flyer ━━━

Bye.

━━━ [2] Weather Girl ━━━

And that is my name, by the way.

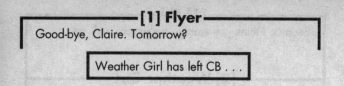

[1] Flyer

Good-bye, Claire. Tomorrow?

Weather Girl has left CB . . .

Eleven

"Nina, get your face out of the mirror," Claire demanded. She struck a three-quarter profile and checked the effects of the foundation on her cheekbones. Then turned and checked the other side. She was in a bra and panties, while Nina wore a robe. *Claire's* robe, of course, lifted from the hook on the back of the bathroom door.

"It's my mirror, too." Nina leaned into Claire, pushed her, and captured several additional inches of the bathroom mirror.

"By the way, excellent cosmetic technique," Claire said snidely. "You could quit school and get a job preparing corpses for burial." Whatever had happened to the good old days when Nina spent Saturday nights lurking in the house watching *Dr. Quinn: Medicine Woman,* and Claire had the bathroom to herself?

"Preparing corpses? Could I practice on you?" Nina casually swiped Claire's mascara.

"Don't *touch* my mascara, Nina. That's mine. Damn it, Nina, you always get the applicator all gummed up." Claire rolled her eyes and made a little guttural noise in her throat that was a signal of exasperation.

"I'm thinking about getting my nose pierced," Nina said, looking at herself critically, a picture that included the ubiquitous Lucky Strike, already stained with dark lipstick.

"Nose piercing is out," Claire said. "Lip piercing is much cooler."

"No way. Where did you hear that?"

"It was in *Sassy*," Claire lied smoothly. "What you do is pierce both lips, upper and lower. Then you put one earring through both holes."

Nina made a face. "Oh, very cute, Claire."

"Is there some reason you can't go buy your own makeup?" Clair asked irritably. "Is there some reason you have to use mine?"

Nina shrugged. "You have better stuff."

"That's because I don't buy mine in five-gallon jugs at the discount drugstore," Claire said, snatching back her blusher. She made a second grab for her mascara, but Nina was too quick.

"I can't deal with buying makeup at the department stores in the mall," Nina said. "Those Clinique girls scare me. White coats, plastic faces, unnatural thinness." She shuddered. "I see them and I start thinking *Invasion of the Bodysnatchers*. Like they're selling beauty products that contain microscopic organisms that take over your mind. I mean, let me ask you—have you ever seen a Clinique girl eat? Aliens never eat, Clinique girls never eat. Coincidence?"

"Nina, why are you here? You're going out with Benjamin, who couldn't care less what your face looks like. Fortunately for you," she added.

"Hey, let me ask *you* something. Why would you wear a bra like that? I mean, doesn't the lace itch?"

"I'm going to a party. Some people believe it's a

nice idea to dress up for a party. Others," she added dryly, "believe in wearing clown makeup and disguising themselves as street people."

"But who's going to see a bra? Unless there's something going on I don't know about?"

"Nina, there is so much going on that you don't know about I wouldn't know where to start," Claire said. She made another grab for the mascara and this time caught it. "Aha!"

"I'm just saying if no one is going to see it, why not wear something comfortable?"

"Like your Doc Marten's steel-tipped bras and your Woolworths' ten-for-a-dollar pull-'em-up-to-your-ribs panties?"

"Does Doc's make bras now? Damn, I didn't know," Nina said.

"You know, the Felixes' house is pretty big, so maybe we could agree to stay on different floors all night."

"I thought maybe Benjamin and I would just follow you and *Joke* around all night. Are you still going with him, by the way? Aisha said she saw you on the stairs the other day at school giving him the evil eye. I explained it was the only kind of eye you have."

"Would I be going to this party with him tonight if we weren't still seeing each other?" Claire answered evasively.

"I just thought after he and Louise—" Nina let the implication hang.

So. Wonderful. Now it was common knowledge that Jake had slept with Louise Kronenberger. Claire had the strange experience of watching her own face in the mirror as she mastered her emotions. A twitch in the muscles of her jaw. A coldness in the narrow-

119

ing of her eyes. "I decided to give him a chance to make it up," Claire said smoothly. "You should be grateful."

"Why should *I* be grateful?"

"Because I don't know all that many guys, really. Jake, Christopher, Lucas . . . Benjamin. If I broke up with Jake, I might have to take one of *them*." She turned a cool, confident stare on Nina. "And Benjamin and I always did get along well."

She'd fully intended the remark to be hard, and even mean, to warn Nina off the topic of Louise permanently. It was a nice little threat that would exploit Nina's insecurity with guys, and Nina's lingering sense of inferiority. It should have backed Nina off like the warning of a rattlesnake.

Except that Nina just laughed. Not a fake-tough laugh, but a genuine, not-worried laugh. "Go ahead and try, Claire. Anytime you want." Then she laughed again.

Claire was startled. She actually took a step back before recovering her composure. "Confident, aren't you?" she said lamely.

Nina nodded. "Yes. See, I don't manipulate Benjamin like you do Jake, so I actually know how he *really* feels. He loves me. I love him."

Claire stopped herself just short of saying *oh yeah?*

Was it her imagination or had Nina grown taller lately? There was definitely something new there. She was still weird Nina, still the annoying, occasionally bizarre Nina. Still the ludicrous unlit cigarette, the permanent bad hair day, the defiantly bad taste in clothing. And yet a different Nina, to be so confident about a guy.

Especially since Claire was confident of so little.

She tried to come up with a suitably clever, biting comeback, but ended up just handing Nina a tissue. "Here," she said. "Your lipstick's smeared there."

Lucas waited and watched like a hawk from the living room of his house. He checked his watch. Seven twenty-five. The ferry was at seven forty, and Aisha hadn't walked past. And yet it was certain that Aisha would pass his house on her way down to meet Christopher and the rest of the gang at the ferry. Christopher intended to surprise them all, especially Aisha, with the truly awful car he'd bought that afternoon.

Except Aisha was notoriously late for everything and she might come tearing by at the last minute at a dead run, which would be no good since he really wanted to talk to her before she saw Zoey.

He really wanted to talk to Aisha. Aisha had seen him on the ferry with Claire on Thursday night. Nothing necessarily fatal there; after all, there were a hundred good reasons why he might have stayed late on the mainland and ended up taking a late ferry home. Same with Claire. There was just the one ferry, and if they had each had separate, perfectly sensible reasons for staying late in Weymouth, well, then, they'd have had no choice but to take the same ferry home.

Right?

Except that talking to Christopher that afternoon had made him nervous. Christopher was of the definite opinion that Zoey would not be understanding. Not at all. And with them all at the same party tonight, crossing on the ferry together, Aisha might just casually blurt something about Thursday night.

Lucas didn't want to have his life ruined by a casual blurt if he could help it.

There she was! Walking past, swinging her arms nonchalantly, wearing sneakers and carrying a pair of leather shoes in her hand, whistling as she went. He jumped up and tore for the door, closing it carefully behind him. His father was a commercial fisherman and was already asleep in preparation for a day that began in the early hours of the predawn.

"Aisha! Hey!"

"Lucas." She stopped and tilted back to give him a critical look. "Looking good, looking good. Haircut?"

"No," he said, panting a little from his burst of speed. "Decided to use a brush."

"Radical," Aisha said.

"Looking forward to the party?"

"I went the last two years," Aisha said. "A cross between a good soap opera and a boxing match."

"Missed them," Lucas said. "What with, you know, being in Youth Authority."

"Too bad. You can't miss Richie Felix's birthday parties. He's kind of a creep, but his parties are great."

Aisha seemed in a much better mood than Lucas had seen her in lately. Downright carefree. Obviously, what Christopher had said was true—the two of them were getting along well. Over the previous few days, especially, it had seemed to Lucas that Aisha had been acting snappish and preoccupied. Come to think of it, she and Christopher had looked half-wasted that night on the ferry. He fell into step with her.

Now he remembered. How many days ago had it been? Hadn't she asked him if he'd helped Christopher buy a gun? Yes, she had asked him that, but he'd been too into his own problems with Zoey to pay much attention—beyond denying it, of course.

"So, Aisha, everything work out okay with you and Christopher the other night? You know, Thursday?" he asked, taking a shot in the dark.

Aisha froze and stared hard at him. "What do you know about that?"

He shrugged.

"It all worked out okay," Aisha said tersely. She pursed her lips and shook her head regretfully. "You know, it would be cool if we could all just kind of forget it, you know? I mean, Christopher's past it now. He doesn't want to talk about it."

Obviously, Lucas noted. He'd spent several hours with Christopher that morning and the dude had said nothing.

Lucas nodded sagely. "Cool by me. Everyone's entitled to a mistake without it having to become gossip of the week." Did that sound too blatantly self-serving?

"Did you tell Zoey about it?" Aisha asked.

"No. Did you?"

"She's a good friend and all," Aisha said, "but this is kind of major stuff. I mean, Christopher could have been arrested, and I don't want people thinking he's some gun-carrying nut. He's not," she added fiercely. "He was tempted, but everyone gets tempted."

"No prob," Lucas said. "As far as I'm concerned I don't know anything." *More true than you know, Aisha,* he added silently, although he was getting some ideas. "In fact, I never even saw you guys on the ferry Thursday night. You weren't there, *I* wasn't there."

Aisha smiled and gave him a quick hug. "You're a good guy, Lucas."

Actually, I'm a low-rent jerk pulling this crap, he reflected. *But whatever it takes.* Christopher was right—this was not the time in Zoey's life when she was going to be understanding about him making out with Claire. Definitely not. But so far this had worked out very nicely. Now, if the rest of the evening just went as smoothly, he'd go on being a happy young man.

Twelve

On the ferry ride from the island to Weymouth they all sat together like the old days, a circle of friends, spread haphazardly around a big part of the upper deck.

Still, Nina realized, things had changed. In the old days she would have been the extra tagalong. She and sometimes Aisha, back before she'd met Christopher. Zoey would have been with Jake, Claire with Benjamin, Lucas . . . well, Lucas would still have been in the Youth Authority. And Nina would have come along as a sort of portable class clown to make jokes and then later to disappear when the couples started making out.

She slipped her left hand into the pocket of Benjamin's jacket. He smiled. She smiled too, foolishly. He found her hand and entwined his fingers with hers. They sat there, some distance apart from the rest, listening to the others talk, Nina stealing secret glances at Benjamin and wishing they weren't with the group because she very, very badly wanted to kiss him.

"We could kind of slip away downstairs," Benjamin whispered.

Nina's smile widened. Evidently Benjamin was thinking along her same lines. Was it true that people in love could read each other's minds? "What would we do down there?"

He shrugged. "Discuss the situation in the Middle East?"

"I'd like that," Nina said huskily. "You know how much I enjoy international relations."

"I guess the others would think it was tacky," Benjamin said, deeply regretful. "It's getting harder and harder being around you."

"Oh, really?" Nina snickered.

Benjamin laughed. "You know what I mean," he whispered. "Stop that," he chided sternly when she kept giggling. "You know perfectly well what I meant was that it's hard being with you and trying to act in a decent, civilized way when what I really want to do is pretty much just make out constantly."

"Me too," Nina said.

"Yeah."

"Uh-huh."

"Hmmm." A sigh.

"The moon came out, by the way," Nina reported, tilting her head back. "It's about half full, shining in a circle with clouds all around. If you want to know precisely what *kind* of clouds, you'll have to ask Claire."

"I don't need to know that badly."

"Good answer," Nina said. It confirmed for her the confidence she'd expressed to Claire. Benjamin *was* over Claire. Really and truly.

"You look beautiful in the moonlight," Benjamin said. "I mean, as I imagine you. The breeze lifting the ends of your hair, your eyes deep in shadow, mysterious but with the light from the stars and the moon reflected there, your lips—''

Nina cleared her throat. ''Claire and Zoey and Aisha would think we were being disgusting if we went downstairs and made out.''

''Yes. All that stuff is supposed to come at the *end* of the date. I mean, if all we do on a date is kiss and so on we might as well have stayed home.''

''You're right. Let's swim back right now.''

Benjamin shook his head. ''Actually, I have kind of a plan for tonight, if you don't mind.''

''A plan?''

''Just a little side trip before we hit the party. It's not exactly a date-type thing. More like a detective-type thing.''

''Oooh. Cool. Then afterward?'' Nina asked.

''After the detective part comes the romance part. That's how it works.''

''And . . . and of course the romance part, that will be the *hard* part.'' Nina began giggling again. ''I tried not to say it, but I couldn't stop myself.''

''I'm very shocked, Nina, really. You are so immature and childish,'' Benjamin said. ''And if I don't get to kiss you within about eight seconds, I may die.''

''Downstairs. You go first. I'll follow in a minute so it will look casual.''

Zoey huddled deeper down in the neck of her sweater and drew her hands up into the sleeves of her coat. It was freezing on the ferry, and her behind was numb from contact with the metal bench. Lucas, Jake, and Christopher were talking about cars, and had been ever since Christopher had revealed his new pride and joy, a car that was frightening even by island standards.

She and Claire were studiously avoiding any conversation at all. Naturally, Claire hadn't apologized for her extraordinary outburst on the stairs Friday, because Claire had almost never been known to apologize for anything. Which left talking only to Aisha, and Aisha was in some kind of waking dream state, humming to herself and occasionally sighing and saying things like "Wow, it's such a beautiful night."

"It's mostly just about horsepower," Jake said.

"I'm just saying with the Viper you've got the horsepower, sure, but that's not the only important thing," Lucas said.

"I'd still rather have a 'Vette," Christopher said.

Claire was looking morose, Zoey observed. She was paying no attention to the guys and instead just focused on some indefinite point in midair. Like she was a million miles away.

She wasn't even paying attention to Nina and Benjamin, who were sitting a little distance away and periodically erupting in giggles.

Zoey couldn't believe how happy Benjamin seemed. How could he? Was he immune to all that was happening to their own family? It almost made her angry; in fact, it did annoy her. It wasn't right. There should be a period of mourning for the death of their family.

"Zero to sixty in less than four seconds," Lucas said.

"That's like you're standing still and then one one-thousand, two one-thousand, three one-thousand, four one-thousand, and boom, you're doing sixty," Christopher offered.

"That would be so excellent," Jake opined.

Zoey noticed that Claire had focused on Nina and Benjamin. There was a bemused expression on her face that gave way slowly to an expression of sadness.

Nina had evidently made some joke, because now Benjamin was laughing, and Zoey bridled at the laughter. How could Benjamin be so cold about what was happening to their parents? To their family? He'd been affected by the spectacle of their father weeping yesterday, but he'd shaken it off in a way that Zoey could not.

Benjamin got up and made his way toward the stairs. Nina fidgeted in a bad parody of indifference for all of about five seconds, then sprang up and went after him.

Claire rolled her eyes and happened to meet Zoey's gaze.

"That was subtle," Claire said dryly.

Zoey managed a weak smile of acknowledgment.

"True love," Claire said with profound sarcasm. "Can't beat it." She looked at Jake, who was entirely engaged with Lucas and Christopher, then looked away again with the sad expression Zoey had noticed earlier.

Zoey looked at Lucas. It hadn't been long since she and Lucas were as nauseating as Benjamin and Nina were now. What had happened to change that?

He had wanted to push their relationship further than she'd been willing to go. That had been the start of it. But she was to blame, too. For neglecting him while she'd become preoccupied with the drama of her parents. He'd asked her—had it only been a couple of days ago?—when she'd spent a sleepless night, still reeling from the worst of the blowup between her parents, whether she still loved him. And she'd said she didn't know.

Yes, there was blame enough to go around. She slipped her cold hand over his. He turned away from Jake and looked at her in surprise. She smiled. He squeezed her hand.

At that moment Jake fell silent. His eyes met Zoey's and Zoey looked away. Claire turned sharply to look out at the dark sea. And floating up from the lower deck came a pearly laugh, suddenly smothered, then renewed an octave lower and quieted again.

"What are we looking at?" Benjamin asked.

"We are looking at a four-story building, Benjamin. Red brick, to be precise. On the bottom floor is a musical instrument shop called Strings. Also a little restaurant or coffee shop or something called Downtown Deli," Nina said.

"I'm guessing it's a delicatessen, then."

"I said it was a restaurant, Benjamin," Nina said. "Don't get all technical on me when you haven't even told me what we're doing here."

She watched his mysterious smile grow wider. He'd been acting strange ever since they'd gotten off the ferry and left the others behind. "We are in search of lost sisters," he said.

"Zoey? She's down at . . . Oh. Really?"

He nodded. "I was able to find out her address. This is the place, unless you're playing tricks on me and we're actually standing outside a McDonald's. 729 Independence, apartment 402. She must live on the top floor."

Nina looked up at the highest row of windows. "Four, five, six windows. Two have lights on."

130

"You see an entrance anywhere?"

Nina looked around. "Maybe it's around the back. No, wait, there it is. It's just a little dark, so I didn't see it at first."

"We need a story," Benjamin said. He stroked his chin thoughtfully.

"What kind of a story?"

"A story for why we're wandering around in this apartment building, in case anyone sees us."

"We don't want to just tell people the truth?"

Benjamin pushed his shades back up on his nose. "Not yet. I want to spy out the situation first."

"Cool. I've never spied before," Nina said. "It adds an edge of excitement to my life."

"Mmmm. We say we're looking for Barney and Betty."

"Who are Barney and Betty?"

"You know, the Rubbles. They live next door to Fred and Wilma. But we say they live at 739 Independence. Seven *three* nine. That way, if anyone questions us they'll just go, 'hey, you're in the wrong building, this is seven *two* nine.' "

"Barney and Betty. Cool. Now what?"

"Now we go in. You lead the way."

Nina guided his hand to her arm. "You know what we could do, if anyone asks us what we're doing. I could pretend to be blind, too. Then they'd say 'no wonder you're lost, it's a case of the—' "

" '—the blind leading the blind.' Uh-huh."

Nina led him up to the doorway and gave Benjamin a dirty look, which, naturally, was lost on him. "You know how long I've waited to be able to use that line? The blind leading the blind. For years I've waited for the right setup." She tried the door and it opened. Inside, a stairwell leading straight up. "Stairs."

They climbed carefully. "Okay, we're on the second floor. Swing around right and we have another flight."

"What's it like in here? Smells like someone's been cooking with curry. I hate curry."

"What's curry taste like?"

"Like curry, Betty," Benjamin said.

"Very funny, Barney. Okay, swing right again and we have still more stairs."

"Someone's coming," Benjamin hissed. "I just heard a door open up on the next floor. Run up ahead and see if you can tell which door. I'm going back down to the second floor."

Nina raced up the rest of the stairs and craned her neck around the corner. A guy and a girl were just coming out of one of the apartment doors. The guy was cute in a scruffy garage-band kind of way. He had major David Pirner hair. Nina's first thought on seeing the girl was that she looked familiar. Probably she'd seen her around on the streets. Nina went past this area twice a day on school days.

The girl spotted her. "Looking for something?" she asked, sounding a bit belligerent.

"Um, yeah. The uh, um, Fred and Barney. I mean, Barney and what's her name. Wilma. Betty. Barney and Betty."

"Not on this floor," the guy said sarcastically. "Try Bedrock."

He and the girl brushed past. "Yeah, Bedrock, ha ha," Nina said. "They hear that all the time."

The couple disappeared down the stairs. Nina ran over to the apartment they'd just left. 402. So, it *was* Benjamin and Zoey's half-sister. Unless Benjamin had the wrong apartment. Or unless these were people who'd been visiting the people who actually lived in the apartment.

She waited till the couple was down the stairs, then ran after them. She found Benjamin at the far end of the second-story hallway, pretending to examine a fire extinguisher.

"Hey, it's them," Nina announced breathlessly. "At least I think it is."

"Where are they now?"

"Should be down to the street by now," Nina said.

Benjamin grinned. "Then the game's afoot!"

"A foot?"

"The game's afoot! Haven't you ever read Sherlock Holmes? Whenever something major's happening, Sherlock says it to Dr. Watson and off they go."

"The game's afoot!" Nina repeated.

"Except I'm Sherlock. So I get to say it. Let's go before they get away."

Nina led him quickly down the stairs and they burst out onto the street. Nina looked left and right, then spotted the couple walking away at an easy pace, arm in arm. "They're heading downtown, back toward Portside. Maybe half a block ahead of us."

"Okay, we follow. But try and be cool about it. Don't let us get too close."

"No prob, Sherlock." Fortunately, the Saturday night street traffic was fairly heavy, with the pedestrians growing thicker as they got closer to the fashionable Portside district.

"What does she look like?" Benjamin asked.

"I just saw her for a few seconds," Nina said. "Brown hair."

"I have brown hair," Benjamin said thoughtfully.

"No, you don't, you have blond hair," Nina said, lying automatically.

Benjamin sighed patiently.

"Okay, she has brown hair, a little lighter than yours. Lots of it, kind of a trashy, puffed-up do. Blue eyes, I think."

"Zoey has blue eyes," Benjamin observed thoughtfully.

"She's tallish. Dresses kind of bar-slutty, no offense if she is your half-sister. I'm seeing a very short mini and cowboy boots."

"You don't approve?"

"A mini with boots? Please. It's a major fashion *don't*. I think I read it in *Glamour*. Oops. They're stopping to look in a window. Here, sit." She pulled him down beside her on a wooden bench. "Look innocent. I have an idea." She grabbed his face and kissed him.

"That's how you look innocent?" he asked wryly.

"There they go. Up. Darn, I can't really see them now in the crowd."

"Damn."

"I'll continue leading you in the same direction they were going in," Nina said carefully. "But since I can't really see them . . . it's almost a case of the blind leading the blind. Ha!"

"Are you happy now?"

"Ha!"

Thirteen

"She told me to walk this way," Jake sang.

"Talk this wa-a-ay," Lucas chimed in.

Zoey and the rest heard the party before they had even turned the last corner onto the street, Aerosmith almost vibrating the pavement underfoot. The Felixes had a great three-story town house right in the Portside neighborhood. Loud music wasn't much of a problem because no one expected to be able to sleep on a Saturday night anyway.

"You know, Richie's a dork," Aisha pointed out, "but the boy does have cool parents."

"Cool?" Christopher said, disbelieving. "They're way past cool. They must be deaf."

"They won't be there," Zoey explained. "Richard has these parties a couple of times a year. His folks check into a hotel for the night and hire a bouncer to make sure things don't get out of hand."

"No way." Christopher laughed.

"A very strange family," Jake said, mercifully cutting short his singing career. They walked as a group up to the door and huddled on the steps. Jake rang the doorbell.

"Like anyone's going to hear the doorbell," Claire pointed out.

But the door opened, letting out a blast of music and revealing a man with a wild mane of blond hair and a build like a professional football player. Behind him was a tall, leggy woman with blue eyes and a skeptical, downturned smile.

"Hi," Zoey said brightly.

"Yeah, whatever," the man said sourly.

The two of them brushed past without another word and headed down the street.

"Looks like the bouncer just took off," Christopher said.

"No, they're Richie's parents," Zoey explained.

They had left the door conveniently ajar, so Jake led the way inside.

A dark entryway opened onto a hallway, which in turn ran past several rooms and eventually on to the kitchen at the back of the house. An open stairway led from the hallway.

In the entryway: people. On the stairs: people. In each of the rooms as Zoey made her way along the hallway: more people. Everywhere people, low lights, loud music, shouted conversation. The last room on the right held a bed piled four feet high with coats. The kitchen held a fifty-gallon Rubbermaid trash can filled with ice studded with bottles of Coke and Mountain Dew. There was a table loaded down with crackers, cheese, brownies, chips and dip, all fairly well destroyed.

Richie appeared suddenly behind Zoey, startling her.

"Thanks for coming!" he shouted.

Zoey nodded. "Wouldn't miss it."

"Hey, you seen my parents?"

"They just left." Zoey pointed back toward the door, hoping sign language would help.

"Excellent." He grabbed Tad Crowley, who was walking by carrying a small stack of CDs. "Tad. The 'rents are out of here. Bring in the keg."

Zoey looked around for Lucas, but they had all been split up in the tide of bodies in motion, pulled away by friends or just the tidal surge. She saw Jake reach for a Coke.

"Brew's on its way," Richie told Jake.

Jake shook his head, and Richie shrugged and went off in pursuit of a girl Zoey didn't recognize.

Jake leaned close to Zoey in order to be heard. "I think I'd better be a good boy and stick to the legal stuff."

Zoey nodded.

"Where'd everyone go?"

Zoey shrugged. She tried an answer, but now it was the Butthole Surfers and the already loud music rose another notch. She leaned close to Jake, putting her hand on his muscular shoulder for balance. "I think I saw Aisha and Christopher heading upstairs. I don't know about the rest. Too dark to see."

"If *you* want a beer, go ahead," Jake said. His lips actually brushed Zoey's ear. Two junior guys came racing through and nearly bumped into Zoey. Jake pulled her out of the way, his hand casually on her waist. He didn't remove his hand. Zoey didn't take her own hand from Jake's shoulder.

"I don't drink very often," Zoey said.

Jake made a self-deprecating face. "I think I may have a problem with alcohol, you know? So I better play it safe. Last time I got drunk at a party I ended up . . ." He prudently let that drop. "Wouldn't want to do anything stupid. Or even say anything stupid."

"Everyone says stupid things," Zoey said dismissively.

For a frozen moment Jake's expression became somber. His serious dark eyes met hers with a look of confusion, hesitation. His mouth opened as if he were going to speak, then he clamped it shut, literally biting his lower lip.

Suddenly he drew his hand away. Just as quickly Zoey took her hand from his shoulder.

"Well, I guess I'd better go find Claire!" he shouted, no longer standing so near as to be heard easily.

"And me, Lucas. I mean, I'd better go find Lucas." She threaded her way from the kitchen and along the hallway, miming hellos as she went, pretending to be able to hear shouted greetings and shrugging at shouted questions. At the foot of the stairs she turned and looked back. Jake was alone, as if an invisible force field kept him apart from the crowd surrounding him. He was looking down, shaking his head slowly.

Zoey climbed the stairs and nearly ran into Lucas, who was coming down at the same moment.

"Hey, I was looking for you," he said.

"I was looking for you, too."

He took her arm and drew her back upward. "Come upstairs; it's a little less loud."

Zoey followed him up and the intensity of the music did diminish somewhat, at least enough that screaming was no longer necessary. Upstairs were several bedrooms feeding off a central hallway. One room reeked of pot smoke. Louise Kronenberger poked her head out, a joint hanging from her mouth. She held it out for Zoey.

"Don't think so, Louise," Zoey said.

Louise giggled happily. "Come on, Zoey, it might

loosen you up. You might actually have fun.''

''Louise, Louise, Louise, haven't you ever seen the egg and the frying pan commercial?'' Lucas said, joking.

Louise pointed to her head. ''Over easy.''

Zoey shook her head. ''More like hard-boiled.''

Louise giggled. ''Zoey made a funny.'' An invisible hand drew her back into the room.

Lucas crooked his finger at Zoey. ''The relatively normal people seem to be down here.''

Zoey bridled. Louise's snide remark about loosening up had rankled a little. Now Lucas was leading her where? To the boring room? To be with the normal people? She grabbed his arm and stopped him in the hallway.

''Am I boring, Lucas?''

He gave her a deprecating look. ''Why, because you don't get high? I don't get high, either.''

''I don't do lots of things,'' Zoey said.

Lucas shrugged dismissively, but Zoey noted he hadn't exactly denied what she was implying.

''I wonder sometimes if maybe you'd be happier with a girl who was more, you know—''

''More like Louise? I had a shot at Louise, remember? No big accomplishment, since basically every guy in school has a fair shot at Louise, but I blew her off.''

''Okay, some other girl,'' Zoey said. ''What if we're not right for each other?''

Lucas's smile disappeared. ''What are you saying?''

''Nothing, I was just thinking maybe I kind of hold you back. Maybe you'd be happier if I weren't your girlfriend.'' It had started as a teasing, nonserious conversation, but now it was deadly earnest.

"Zoey, I love *you*. Not some other girl." He glanced around self-consciously, lest some male overhear him.

"I love you, too, Lucas," Zoey said. She felt troubled, like she was sliding down a long, slippery slope, but she couldn't stop now. "But you must look at other girls sometimes."

"Of course I *look*," Lucas said. "Everyone *looks*. That doesn't mean anything."

"When you see other girls, don't you sometimes think, I'll bet she'd be easier to get along with than Zoey is?"

"Only when you're having PMS," Lucas said.

"I'm serious. Don't you think, I'll bet that girl would be more fun, or more cool, or maybe she's prettier, or maybe she'd, you know, have sex?"

Lucas's eyes narrowed. "Are you saying this because you're thinking about other guys?"

"Of course not."

"Like maybe you're thinking some other guy has more money or has a cool car or maybe this other guy wouldn't be trying to pressure me into sleeping with him?"

"We were talking about *you*," Zoey said impatiently. "About what you want."

"I want you," he said simply.

"Just me?" She looked searchingly at his face.

His eyes darted away, then returned to meet hers defiantly. "Just you, Zoey."

"It's important for me to know, Lucas. To be absolutely sure. I mean, sometimes people seem like everything's okay, like they're a happy couple and all that, then you find out that's not the way it was."

"You mean like your parents?"

Zoey nodded in mute acknowledgment. Of course

that's what she meant, although she hadn't been thinking about it consciously.

"You know, maybe your dad really does still love your mom and she loves him. I mean, maybe it was just one of those things that happened."

"Just happened? My mother just happened to sleep with another man?"

"There was a lot of history there," Lucas pointed out. "She'd just found out your dad had a kid by some other woman nineteen years ago and never even told her. She was pissed. She wanted to get her pride back after the way your dad treated her."

"Yeah, she really has her pride now," Zoey sneered.

"People do stupid things they're sorry for later," Lucas said. He looked down at the floor and shook his head, reminding Zoey of Jake.

"Don't expect me to forgive her," Zoey said. "If two people supposedly love each other, they don't do things like that, betraying the other person behind their back."

"Maybe you're wrong," Lucas said earnestly. "Maybe that is the way people are."

"Then they're jerks," Zoey said harshly. "I would never do that to you."

"No, I guess you wouldn't."

"This looks serious," Christopher said, passing by.

Lucas looked relieved. "No, no, just talking."

"I lost Aisha in here somewhere."

"Here I am." Aisha appeared and wrapped her arms around Christopher from the back. "Let's go downstairs and dance. The DJ said he'd do some dance tunes."

"You guys want to come?" Christopher asked.

"Maybe in a little while," Lucas said.

"I guess I'm being kind of a drag, huh?" Zoey said. "Sorry. This whole divorce thing has kind of preoccupied me."

"I understand," Lucas said.

"We're not my parents," Zoey said. "I do understand that. I mean, it's stupid to start being suspicious about everyone. Especially you." She slipped her arms around his sides and pressed against him.

Lucas kissed her.

Fourteen

"The Portside Tavern," Nina said. "They just went inside."

Benjamin paused to consider. "What's it like inside?"

"I've never been in there," Nina admitted. "Supposedly it's kind of funky. They serve food and all. Plus there's a band, I think."

"Maybe we wouldn't be too conspicuous." He didn't sound convinced.

"Yeah, a high school junior and a blind guy in the Portside Tavern, that wouldn't attract any attention," Nina said.

"Okay, look. How about if you park me somewhere and you go in. See what they're up to in there. Probably just drinking or whatever. Listening to music."

Nina felt a little nervous at the prospect of leaving Benjamin out on the street alone on a Saturday night, but there was no way to mention it that wouldn't just make him mad. "Okay. Do a one-eighty. About four steps. There's a bench."

She waited until Benjamin was seated, looking very casual behind his shades though she could see the tension in the way he crossed his legs. *Tense at being out alone on a rowdy street*? she wondered. More likely just excited by all the detective play-acting. That was Benjamin, she realized fondly. The boy did love a mystery he could pick at.

She went through the front door of the Portside. Fortunately, there was no bouncer since it was still early in the night and the big crowds wouldn't be along for an hour or so.

The room had a low ceiling and bare brick walls that made it feel like you were in someone's base-ment. There was no band, just recorded music. Bad music, Nina noted.

The restaurant area was partly full, but most of the people were crowded around the bar. Including Lara and her presumed boyfriend, the guy with the hair. From the way the bartender greeted them, it was obvious they were known here. One of the cock-tail waitresses went over and said hi to Lara. The boyfriend—Mr. Hair, as Nina thought of him—gave the waitress's butt an appreciative look.

Drinks appeared. Lara and Mr. Hair tossed them back like pros. Two more appeared. These went down just as quickly. Then Mr. Hair went off with the cocktail waitress in the direction of the kitchen. Lara didn't seem at all concerned. In fact, she barely seemed to notice.

Nina realized she was standing around looking ex-posed and obvious. She decided to head toward the ladies' room like she was on a mission. As she passed by, Mr. Hair and the waitress emerged from the kitchen. The waitress went straight toward the bathroom, entering just behind Nina.

Now that she was in the bathroom, Nina decided she'd better look as normal as possible. She took one stall while the waitress took the other. While Nina made the experience as realistic as possible, she listened and heard small crackling sounds from the next stall—tin foil or plastic wrap maybe. Probably opening a tampon, she decided.

Then there was a sniffing sound, unusually prolonged. A sneeze. A curse. A long sniffing sound again.

Nina flushed and left quickly. Lara and Mr. Hair seemed to be ready to go. Both refused another drink from the genial bartender. Mr. Hair reached across and shook the bartender's hand. The bartender gave him a wink and went on about his business.

Nina fell into step a few feet behind the couple. Outside she found Benjamin on the bench, still looking very casual, calmly gazing around as if he was interested in the people passing by. It would have taken a close observer to notice that his gaze never exactly followed anyone or focused on anything especially interesting, but instead was frequently aimed at a section of blank wall.

"Let's go, Holmes," she hissed. "The game's feet are heading across the street."

"What did you find out?" Benjamin asked, taking her arm.

What had she learned? Nothing exactly, although she was having the beginning of a suspicion. "Not much. They had a couple of drinks. Mr. Hair—"

"Mr. Hair?"

"The boyfriend."

"Oh."

"Mr. Hair goes off with one of the waitresses for like a minute, then the waitress goes to the john, where she was either trying to inhale tampons or doing a couple lines of coke. Could be crank. Or it could be NeoSynephrine and she has a stuffed-up nose."

Benjamin nodded thoughtfully. "The way you describe it, it could be coincidence."

"Yeah, I know. Also, he shook the bartender's hand."

"A long handshake? A handshake that made you think 'hmm, there's something significant in that handshake'?"

"A handshake that made me think 'hey, that guy's slipping that bartender something he doesn't want anyone else to see.'"

"And they were both drinking, right?"

"Bada boom, straight down the throat, no waiting," Nina confirmed.

"Yeah. Interesting. Lara's only nineteen, supposedly. Shouldn't be able to drink in a bar like that. Unless she knows someone."

"Ah, excellent point, Sherlock."

"Where are we heading now?" Benjamin asked. "By my count we're just down from the Chickenlips Saloon."

"And they just went inside. I'm on them. Here, squat down."

"Squat down?" he echoed.

"Squat. You're reading the front page of the newspaper through the front of the machine."

Nina left him and ran to catch up. Here, unfortunately, the bouncer was already on duty, and there was no chance that Nina was going to pass for twenty-one. She rejoined Benjamin.

"Doorman," she explained.

"Damn." He stood up. "It doesn't matter. If they come out in less than ten minutes, we'll have a pretty good idea."

As it happened, they emerged in just over five minutes.

"Off we go," Nina said.

"One more try, after that we drop it," Benjamin said. "I mean, it's night and we're trailing a guy we think may be a dealer. Some people would say that's not all that brilliant."

"Lots of people would say that."

Benjamin frowned. "Wait, unless I'm way off, there aren't any more bars on this street. From here on up it's residential, isn't it?"

"Yeah. You guessed it."

"Well, well. What a coincidence."

Claire danced with Jake

Claire was a precise, elegant dancer, always carefully understated, never wild. She could stay on the beat, but she gave no impression that the music affected her on an emotional level. Possibly because it did not in fact affect her much one way or the other. For Claire, dancing was a duty, something she had to do, like saying hello to people or laughing politely at people's jokes or any of the countless other basically irrelevant things she had to do to get along. She was determined to do well since it was unthinkable that she would ever be a dweeb. And it was a part of that duty to project a certain subtle sexuality, and so she did that, too. Still, the impression she gave was of a person who would be every bit as pleased to be reading a book, which was literally true.

Jake danced with more grace than people expected of someone with so much muscle, with legs as hard and big around as fire hydrants and shoulders that seemed to extend an unnatural distance in either direction. There was grace, but sheer size limited his movements, so that he danced carefully, always aware of people around him who might not want to be struck by a carelessly swung arm. In his own mind he looked like a dancing bear straight out of the circus, but at least, as dancing bears went, he was one of the more gentle ones.

Aisha danced with Christopher

Aisha was not exactly embarrassing as a dancer, but close to it. She believed that underneath it all, dance was surely somehow a mathematical exercise that could be figured out by means of formulas—foot goes here and hand goes there. Hip out as arm moves down. This would work for as much as thirty seconds at a time, before the system would break down and she would come to an almost complete stop before trying a new variation. Her usual expression was one of concentration, succeeded sooner or later by frustration.

♫

Christopher danced like a fugitive from MTV's *The Grind*. He was all liquid, effortless control, not just responding to the music but instinctively anticipating it, knowing what came next, there before it happened. Inventive without being showy. Athletic without being extreme.

In fact, he knew full well he could be much better, but there was nothing to be gained by making other people look bad. Especially people who thought dancing was secretly a form of algebra.

Zoey danced with Lucas

Zoey danced small, almost shyly. She was a good dancer, but not innovative or demonstrative. Mostly she did what others did, kept her eyes on Lucas or on the floor, because looking into someone's eyes when you were gyrating provocatively was dorky. She was sorry that Benjamin wasn't here, because when he danced people mostly paid attention to him, unable to believe he could be so cool without being able to see. At least Claire was dancing, which guaranteed that most of the guys would be looking at her and not at Zoey.

Lucas hated dancing with all his heart. If he could just never dance, he would be happy. Someday, when he was in a steady relationship and didn't have to do the whole dating thing anymore, he would simply stop. When he was married, he would never go dancing. Never. Not for money. Not with a gun to his head. But it was a basic part of high school dating life, and he didn't quite have the nerve to just say no. He was jealous of people like Nina, whom he'd seen dancing at homecoming. Nina could just spaz out, totally lost to reality while she was dancing. Lucas was trapped in reality. The reality that he felt like the largest, most obvious dweeb on the planet when he had to dance.

Fifteen

Claire knew it was perfectly natural and normal and to be expected that eventually Jake would dance with Zoey. It would have been strange if he hadn't. They were friends, after all. Besides, everyone traded partners during the course of a party. Only the most insanely jealous couples got upset at seeing their dates dance with someone else. It was even to be expected that guys might flirt with other girls, or girls with guys. That was all a part of life, especially at a party.

The problem was that while Jake and Zoey danced, neither of them flirted. It was a strange thing to be upset over, Claire acknowledged privately, and yet she was upset.

Jake was behaving with unnatural rigidity around Zoey. He was stiff and formal, not a smile or a laugh. Yet when Zoey was distracted by a girl she knew and turned away from him for a moment, Jake's eyes were on her, following Zoey's every movement. Not the usual check-out-her-butt glance. Nothing that crude and harmless. Instead he looked at her with a wistful longing, the way a person looked at something he had loved and lost and wished he could have again.

The DJ played a slow song, the G 'n R cover of *Since I Don't Have You.* Claire almost laughed. Perfect. Zoey was with Jake, looking around nervously, like maybe she shouldn't do a slow dance with him. Jake was standing there awkwardly, big arms at his sides, looking half-hopeful, half-afraid.

At that moment Claire believed she might actually hate him. He so wanted to take Zoey in his arms and dance with her. He so desperately wanted her to let him hold her.

Claire turned away, afraid she would lose her composure completely. She couldn't bear the thought that Zoey might look over and realize she was upset. She felt a sickening twisting in her stomach.

When Claire looked back, they were dancing. Both holding each other at a safe distance, Zoey smiling politely, uncomfortable but determined to act as if everything was normal. Jake . . . Jake looked like a big, stupid puppy who'd stolen a bone from the table and was beside himself with joy yet fearful his prize might be snatched away.

Claire tried not to look, but she couldn't help herself. There it was in Jake's face, the proof. Of course he still loved Zoey. Had there ever been a time, even for a minute or two, when he didn't? Had there been a minute or two in there when he had genuinely loved Claire?

How would she ever know? Claire asked herself. Her whole relationship with Jake had been born of her own careful manipulation. It had all been very clever on her part. Wonderfully intelligent, far outclassing poor Jake's efforts to resist her.

Only now, underneath it all, it was still Zoey he wanted. Zoey, who had kept ownership of his heart by turning on him and choosing Lucas.

She wondered idly how Lucas would feel about this, but that was pointless. Zoey had done nothing blameworthy in his eyes.

No, that wasn't the way to handle this at all. There was another way. A cold, ruthless, but effective way to take care of Jake's puppy love for Zoey.

It wouldn't make him love Claire. She was now prepared to accept that at least that was impossible. But it would ruin his little fantasy for a long while.

Jake released Zoey at the end of the short, too short song. Lucas had come back on the floor, and Zoey had let him put his arms around her. Jake's own arms felt empty now. He managed a smile for Lucas, an acknowledgment as close to graciousness as he was capable of.

It would have been uncool to say one tenth of what he felt. Hopelessly uncool to express the way he still felt when he saw Zoey with Lucas. A man didn't act that way, and Jake was a man.

He looked around for Claire and saw her not far off, a pale, solitary figure that stood out from the crowd as if she were lit with her own personal spotlight. Beautiful, smart, strong Claire. She was the girl every guy in school fawned over. There were plenty who would toss their present girlfriends aside for half a chance at Claire. And she was *his* girlfriend. He was lucky; everyone said so.

"Hey, babe," he said. He put his arm around her waist just as Lucas had done with Zoey.

And Claire smiled, just as Zoey had smiled for Lucas.

"I missed you," she said.

"Me too," he said, trying to sound as if he meant it.

"Kiss me," Claire said.

He did. How could he not? And her lips were soft beyond belief, her mouth so sensual and inviting. And yet he felt as though Zoey must be watching them. In a way he hoped she was watching and feeling at least the smallest amount of jealousy.

"Let's go upstairs," Claire said, in her voice that accepted no argument. "I'm tired of all this noise."

She took his hand and led him away from the dance floor and up the stairs, past the second floor to the third. The third floor was far enough away from the speakers to be relatively quiet. Most of it was semi-finished attic, with a wood floor and no partitions. Exercise equipment was scattered at one end, weights and an Exercycle and a Soloflex. At the other end of the room was a pool table, where no fewer than six people were wielding cues.

The exercise end of the room was darker, lined with dormered windows and inset benches. It was to one of these that Claire led Jake.

"Reminds me of—" Jake began, before deciding he'd better not go on.

"Zoey's bedroom?" Claire supplied. "Yes, I always liked that desk she has built into her window."

They sat together, facing each other, both with a leg kicked up onto the bench. Claire's skirt slipped up her leg. She swept her silken black hair back over her shoulder and looked at him with a frank, appraising expression.

"We're all alone now, more or less," Claire suggested.

He nodded. There was something wrong with this situation. On its surface Claire had just brought him up here to make out. Plenty of other couples were doing the same thing—and more—at various locations around the house.

Except that Claire didn't do things like this. Jake felt alarm bells going off, but what could he do? Claire leaned into him, glittering dark eyes closing ever so slowly, her lush lips open.

She kissed Jake with an intensity he had never known from her. She left him gasping for air. His heart was racing. Almost against his will a sly smile spread over his face. "That was nice," he admitted.

"Well, I like kissing you," Claire said.

"I like kissing you, too," Jake said truthfully. Whatever fantasies he harbored about Zoey, Claire was here, now, very close. Claire could kill at a hundred yards; this close she was irresistible. Even when he had been so haunted by the memory of what she had done to his brother, Jake had never been able to build up any sort of immunity to her.

Claire kissed him again, then pulled away, leaving him leaning forward into emptiness. She laid her hand on his face. "I guess our relationship has reached a point where we can be honest about how we feel," Claire said thoughtfully.

"I guess so." Again the warning bells, but softer, more confused this time.

"Well, look, Jake, I don't want to lose you, but I think it's time we cleared up some stuff that I may not have been totally honest about." She turned to look out of the window, her face lit by moonlight.

"Sounds major," Jake said jokingly.

She shrugged. "It is and it isn't. Of course you know that I know about you and Louise Kronenberger," she said. "You know, that you slept with her. Had sex with her."

Jake shifted uncomfortably. "Look, Claire, I was drunk, and I mean really, really drunk. Plus, you know about the whole thing that was going on then—I'd been doing drugs earlier that night, and the game, and getting suspended. And we weren't exactly going together, you and me, not really."

Claire made a wry smile. "I know there were mitigating circumstances. And I'm not blaming you. Not at all. I'm just saying since I know about you, it seems unfair for me not to tell you my little secret."

Jake swallowed. He gave her a hard, suspicious look. "What do you mean?"

"Well, it turns out I'm not exactly a virgin, either, Jake." She smiled like they were conspirators.

He froze. He had been right to hear warning bells. "Who was the . . . who did you do it with?"

Claire smiled impishly, an unnatural look for her. She was enjoying this. "Who do you think?"

"Benjamin?"

"No, not Benjamin." She laughed, as though that was somehow a funny suggestion. "Like I'd sleep with my sister's boyfriend; give me some credit. That would be way too *Oprah*. Of course not Benjamin."

"Do you mean this was—like recently?"

"Now don't get upset," Claire said.

"I just want to know, that's all," Jake demanded, his voice rising.

"Lucas."

"Lucas?"

Claire tried out the impish smile one more time. She added an insouciant shrug. "You have to admit he is kind of cute."

Jake looked like he'd been punched in the stomach. He was dazed and breathless. "You slept with Lucas. Like a long time ago, when you guys were going together?"

"It was just a couple of days ago," Claire said. "I mean, it was just fun. I'm not in love with him or anything. It was just sex. You know, like you and Louise."

"I didn't even remember that, Claire!"

"Sorry," Claire said huffily. "I didn't know that made it any different. I *do* remember." Now, she told herself—just the smallest little smile, eyes averted, like I'm remembering. A coy little smile that will eat at him forever.

She saw the shocked anger in Jake's eyes. And then, following the first emotion, came the slow dawning of calculation. Just as she had known it would. His next question would be . . .

"Am I supposed to believe this is all okay with Zoey?"

She could almost have slapped him at that moment. But that would have been a superficial, temporary pain. "You know how straight Zoey is," she said. "She'd never be able to deal with it. Lucas didn't tell her, obviously."

"And you think I *can* deal with it?"

No, Claire said silently. *I don't think for a moment that you can deal with it. I think you'll never want to touch me again, believing that I slept with Lucas.* "What's the big deal?"

"What's the big deal?" Jake nearly screamed.

"Oh, it's okay if you sleep with Louise, but it's not okay if I do it with Lucas? You might try being a little more consistent, Jake." No more cuteness now. It was no longer necessary to be coy. The damage was done. "Not being sexist, are you? Okay for guys, but not okay for girls?"

"How could you do that to Zoey? And to me?"

She looked at him coldly, letting some small part of her inner rage peek through. "How could I do that to you, Jake?" Claire realized she was trembling now. The playacting was over with. She got to her feet. "Don't play high-and-mighty with me, Jake. You think I'm blind? You think I don't know you still love Zoey? And don't you think Lucas suspects the same about her?"

Ah, his eyes actually lit up at the possibility! Even now, he couldn't help it. So much the better. He deserved what he was getting.

"Lucas and I know all about your ever-so-chaste ongoing love affair. So we decided to have a little fun of our own." She leaned down close to Jake's face. "And it was fun, Jake. Lucas was wonderful. As Zoey will find out sooner or later, when she gets over playing junior nun."

Jake shot to his feet, bristling with rage and horror. "You bitch." His hands clenched into fists, but Jake wasn't the kind to strike out at her, no matter how outraged he was. Besides, beneath it all, he was constructing a whole new world of hope.

She watched as he walked stiffly away.

Damn him to hell. She was well rid of any guy stupid enough to fall for this cheap trick. Benjamin would never have fallen for it. Not Benjamin. Benjamin who, like the others, no longer loved her.

Claire threw herself back onto the bench and, in the privacy of the dark recess, cried tears of bitter self-loathing.

Sixteen

His brand-new half-sister, was, in all likelihood, a drug dealer. Or, if not a drug dealer herself, then involved with one. She couldn't possibly be ignorant of what Mr. Hair was up to. Not unless she was an idiot. And so far no one in the family had turned out to be an idiot.

"You realize where they're going," Benjamin said.

"Duh. I mean, it's a good guess, anyway," Nina said.

"And can we possibly guess *why* they would be going to Richie Felix's birthday party?" Benjamin asked sourly. The music from the party was clearly audible. Bass was vibrating up through the cobble-stones.

"They like to dance?" Nina suggested.

"Uh-huh. You know, I kind of feel like I don't really want to know who they're selling drugs to at this party. I mean, it's all people from school, people we know."

Nina made a doubtful noise. "I thought you wanted to know everything, Sherlock. There they go, by the way. Right inside. Didn't even bother to knock."

"Not always. I mean, do I want to know what kids at school are using drugs? Not really. Besides, I don't want to spy on *them*. I just wanted to see if I could get some answers about my alleged half-sister; you know, get a sense of things before I decide whether to meet her face to face."

"This is so *The Young and the Restless*," Nina said. "Half-sisters. Drug dealers. You are going to talk to her eventually, aren't you?"

Benjamin considered the question as they closed the distance to the Felix house. "I suppose. It's kind of a major decision, though. Let's hold back for a couple of minutes. We don't want to come in right after them. It might look kind of obvious."

"It's cold out here, though," Nina complained.

"Are you dressed warmly?"

"I'm wearing a warm coat, but I have nothing on underneath," Nina said.

He could hear the leer in her voice. Even though he knew she was teasing, the image still sent a pleasurable tingle through him. "Don't say things like that," he said with mock-severity. "Sherlock never had the slightest interest in women."

He felt her settle close to him, sharing his body heat. "I guess it is kind of major," she said thoughtfully. "I mean, not every brother-sister thing is as nice as you and Zoey. Look at Claire and me. We already know this girl's a possible drug dealer. Which means there's a chance she's almost as rotten as Claire."

"It's not just that," Benjamin said. "There's the whole question of how she'll feel about suddenly having an unknown family popping up in the middle of her life. Suddenly she'd have a half-brother and a half-sister and a biological father. Some people would consider that upsetting.''

"You're so thoughtful,'' Nina said affectionately. "I was just thinking she might be the kind of person who'd want to borrow your CDs.''

Benjamin laughed perfunctorily, but his thoughts were elsewhere. "Tell me again what she looks like,'' he asked.

Nina was silent.

"Are you there?'' Benjamin prodded.

He heard Nina sigh. "Benjamin, I don't know whether or not she looks like you. She might, I guess, but I can't be sure.''

"Oh. Was I being that obvious?''

"No, it's just that I know the way your twisted, devious mind works. You're thinking maybe your mom and dad lied to you?''

"Their record for honesty isn't all that great right now,'' he pointed out.

"Benjamin, you're being dumb. Your mom is your mom and your dad is your dad.''

"Let me ask you something—do I look like my dad at all?''

Nina made a growling frustrated noise deep in her throat. "Okay, you look more like your mom. It's obvious to anyone that you and she look alike. Same nose, same chin.''

"And nothing in common with my father?''

"You're both kind of cute, although he's actually much cuter, you know, if you like old guys.''

"Mmm-hmm. So, the answer is no.''

"Look, you also don't look like Mr. McRoyan, if that's what you're thinking. Not at all. This is dumb. So what if we decide Lara looks like you?''

He shrugged. It did sound a little farfetched.

Maybe it was just the paranoia that came from never being able to see things for himself. "If she looks like me, then I guess I'll conclude that we are related. Meaning we have the same father and that my father is my father."

Nina was silent for a long time. Then, "You're a strange person, Benjamin. I used to think maybe underneath it all we weren't right for each other, that I was too weird or whatever. But you are plenty weird your own self."

"Let's go, Dr. Watson."

"First kiss me, Sherlock," Nina said. "If it turns out Mr. McRoyan *is* your real father, that will make you *Joke's* half-brother. I might not want to kiss anyone related to him."

"Seems pretty peaceful," Nina remarked, looking across the dance floor.

"What?" Benjamin shouted. "If you want me to hear you, you'll have to scream directly into my ear. Someone is landing a jet in here."

"I said it seems peaceful!" Nina yelled.

"Oh, yeah. This is peaceful, all right."

Various kids from school came over and said hello, exchanging unheard jokes and polite laughter. Richie appeared in his characteristically sudden way, startling Nina by patting her on the back. He mouthed words for a while, and Nina nodded and smiled in response.

"What did he say?" Nina asked Benjamin.

"Who? Was someone here?"

"Our host. Richie. He was telling me something. I thought you'd be able to hear with your Blind Boy superhearing."

Benjamin grinned. "I can't use my superpowers

161

unless I'm wearing my Blind Boy costume."

"What's that? A red cape and Calvin Klein briefs?"

Benjamin put on a shocked expression. "A red cape? That's Superman. I'd never infringe on his trademark style. I think Blind Boy's costume should be mismatched plaids and polka dots and stripes."

"I like my idea better," Nina said. "Hey, there's Lucas!" She raised her voice and shouted his name at full volume.

Whether he had heard or just happened to spot them, he came over. "Where have you guys been?"

"We got lost," Nina said. "I let Benjamin try and lead us. We ended up out by the mall."

"Any major excitement yet?" Benjamin asked.

Lucas shook his head. "Nah. Kind of disappointing. I kept hearing how wild and unpredictable these parties are."

"Usually by now we'd have had at least two or three screaming breakups and an equal number of drunken fistfights," Benjamin confirmed.

Nina spotted a familiar head rising up the stairs. She put her mouth to Benjamin's ear. "Mr. Hair, going upstairs."

"We're going to go check things out," Benjamin said. "Is Zoey around?"

"She was just here. Had to go to the little girls' room with Aisha."

Nina led Benjamin to the bottom of the stairs.

Jake took the plastic cup greedily and swallowed the beer in several long gulps. That was five, and he was beginning to feel the buzz, a fiery sensation starting in the muscles of his neck. Tad Crowley was working the tap, draining beer into cups, setting the cups on the kitchen butcher block table.

"Let someone else get one," Tad said, shaking his head in bemusement. "It's a long night, Jake; pace yourself, man."

Lars Ehrlich came up suddenly and popped Jake playfully on the shoulder. He was grinning and pink, but his face grew more cautious when he saw Jake's face. "Hey, big Jake. If you want to get truly hammered, come on upstairs, man. I don't want to share with all these losers."

Jake shook his head resolutely. "No more drugs. I fail a piss test again and I'm history as far as the team is concerned."

"Plus, your dad will kill you," Lars said.

"My dad can go to hell," Jake snapped. "He's no better than anyone else. Worse. Give me another beer," he demanded of Tad. The days of worrying what his father would say or do were over now. They'd been over since he'd learned about his father and Zoey's mom. His father was in no position to judge, not anymore. He was no better than Lucas. The same as Lucas, another behind-the-back cheapshot artist. Lucas had betrayed Zoey, and his father had betrayed his mother. What was the difference?

Lars opened his jacket suggestively. Nestled inside, Jake saw a bottle of clear liquid. "Tequila," Lars said, wiggling his eyebrows. "It'll get you there faster than beer."

"My man, Lars," Jake said magnanimously. He followed Lars upstairs.

They found a corner of one bedroom. A couple was making out without much interest on the bed. Some older-looking guy with lots of hair and a pretty but slightly trashy-looking girl Jake had never seen were in secretive conversation with two of the school's more notorious druggies.

Lars cracked the seal on the bottle, took a swig, shuddered, and handed the bottle to Jake. Jake quickly raised the bottle and took two deep swallows that burned like fire all the way down. The effect was almost immediate. His head swam, and he had to steady himself by reaching out for the windowsill.

"See what I mean?" Lars leered.

But Jake wasn't interested in what Lars had to say. He was interested in wiping the lurid image of Claire with Lucas from his mind. It wasn't that he cared so much about Claire cheating on him. Maybe he even deserved it after Louise. Besides, Jake knew he was no paragon. Maybe once he'd believed he was someone special, but now he knew better.

No, it was Zoey who was special. It was the betrayal of Zoey that hurt. How could Lucas have done it? How could Claire? Both of them not fit to kiss Zoey's shoes. It would tear Zoey up when she found out.

He took another drink. It would tear her up, but at the same time it would be good for her in the long run to be rid of Lucas. Only how would she find out? That was the question—would she ever find out, or would Lucas just go on laughing behind her back?

No, no, no. That couldn't be allowed. The thought that Lucas could have betrayed Zoey and yet still have her all to himself . . . She had to be told. She had to be told the truth. And the sooner the better.

Aisha rummaged through the contents of her purse and finally, in frustration, upended it and dumped the contents onto the marble counter. Her eyeliner rolled into the sink. A pack of gum fell onto the tile floor of the cramped, over bright bathroom.

Zoey bent down to pick it up for her. "Here. Your gum. What are you doing, anyway?" They were crammed into the tiny bathroom together. Actually, the two of them and the girl who was passed out and snoring in the bathtub.

"I'm looking for a tampon. I was sure I had one more in here." Aisha raked through the mess she'd made.

"I'll check my purse," Zoey offered. "Wait, here. No, sorry, that was Lifesavers."

"What flavor?" Aisha asked sarcastically. "I'd rather use peppermint if it comes down to that."

"Passion fruit," Zoey said with a smile. "Hang on, I'll see who's outside." She opened the door a crack and happened to spot Nina and Benjamin walking past.

"Nina," Zoey hissed.

"Hey, Zoey," Nina said. "Benjamin, your sister is here. Peeking out of the bathroom like a spy."

"Hi, Zoey."

"Hi, Benjamin. Um, Benjamin? This kind of just involves Nina," Zoey said.

"Oh, fine. I can take a hint. I'll just stand out here while you girls have all the fun."

Zoey grabbed Nina and yanked her inside, closing the door on Benjamin. "Aisha needs a tampon."

"I'll check," Nina offered. "But I think all I have is my wallet and cigarettes and gum." She extracted a Lucky Strike and popped it into the corner of her mouth. "No, wait, I have Lifesavers, too. Wintergreen." She held up the pack.

Aisha sighed. "We have Lifesavers. I don't need Lifesavers."

"Wait. Aha!" Nina held up the tampon. "What will you pay me?"

Aisha snatched it out of her hand. "You two can leave now."

"Hey, Eesh," Nina said, "I was watching Christopher downstairs dancing. He's good."

"You know how it is, all of us black people can dance."

"Yeah, right. I've seen *you* dance," Nina pointed out. "You know the Tin Man in *The Wizard of Oz*?"

"Please leave now," Aisha said, batting her eyelashes. "Please go away and find someone else to ridicule."

Zoey and Nina slipped outside into the hallway and rejoined Benjamin, who was carrying on a polite conversation with a sophomore girl Nina had seen hanging around him before.

"So what have you two been up to?" Zoey asked.

Benjamin responded by looking uncomfortable. Nina put on her blank look, the one she resorted to when she was avoiding telling the truth. Nina was the lamest liar imaginable.

"Actually, Zoey—" Benjamin began.

"Um, what were we up to?" Nina jumped in. "Nothing. We've been here the whole time, you just didn't see us."

"Nina, I think I might as well tell her," Benjamin said, looking amused but also a little nervous.

"Tell me what?" Zoey asked.

"I, uh, I located our half-sister. You know, Lara? Turns out she lives here in town."

Zoey froze. "Benjamin, what have you done?"

"We followed her. And now, oddly enough, it turns out she's here." He smiled winningly.

Zoey shot a glance at Nina, who just shrugged. "You told her who you are?"

"No," Benjamin said. "I haven't told her."

"You must have told her, Benjamin, or why else would she be here?" Zoey insisted.

"I'm not sure you really want to know *why* Lara's here," Benjamin said in an undertone. "She's here with her boyfriend, and unless we're really out of line somehow, it kind of looks like her boyfriend is in a certain illegal business that involves making a lot of stops around town."

"Damn it, Benjamin," Zoey said. "What made you go off and do this?"

"Chill out, Zoey. I don't take orders from you, *little* sister."

There was a warning edge in Benjamin's voice, but Zoey was too angry to let it go. "This is something that affects both of us, Benjamin. You should have at least asked me."

"It was important to me," Benjamin argued. "I wanted to know who she was and what she was like."

Zoey fought down an angry reply. Throughout the whole mess of the split between their parents, she and Benjamin had managed to stay on the same side, though his feelings differed from hers in some ways. She took a deep breath. "Look, I don't want to fight with you, Benjamin. It just caught me by surprise, all right? A couple of days ago I suddenly learn I have this so-called half-sister, then you cruise in and say, 'Oh, by the way, she's here at the party and I think she deals drugs.' "

Benjamin made a wryly sympathetic face. "You're saying that's what? Kind of a surprise?"

"Yeah," Zoey said. She smiled, too, and saw

Nina relax. "You're not going to introduce yourself, are you?"

"No. Not yet," he said. "Knowledge is power. For now I'm happy knowing who she is without her knowing anything about me, or us."

Zoey considered, curiosity warring with caution. Curiosity won. "Okay, so where is she?"

Nina pointed to a doorway just down the hall. "Tall, brown hair, not bad looking but slightly sleazy. She's with a guy who looks like David Pirner."

"David Pirner?" Benjamin asked.

"Lead singer for Soul Asylum," Nina clarified. "Jeez, Benjamin, enter the nineties."

Zoey rolled her eyes. "I'm just going to take a peek."

"See what you think of her," Benjamin said seriously. "Take a good look at her."

Zoey started toward the door, feeling faintly ridiculous playing games. She looked in the door. There was a couple making out on the bed. There were two guys in the shadows of the far corner of the room. Just inside the door, two more guys she knew from school were huddled close to a couple, an older guy with lots of hair, and a girl.

Zoey just took a glance and turned away. So that was her half-sister. Had she looked like a relative? She'd have to get a closer look.

Only now the two of them, Lara and her boyfriend, were leaving, brushing past without apparently seeing her. And at the same time, just over their shoulders, Zoey had recognized one of the two people sharing a bottle of liquor.

Seventeen

"Damn, here come Lara and Mr. Hair," Nina hissed. She grabbed Benjamin's arm and propelled him down the hallway. Unfortunately Marie Burnett was blocking their way, asking Nina something about Modern Media class.

"Hey, it's that same girl," Mr. Hair said.

"What is with Mr. Mifflin lately?" Marie wanted to know. "I mean, quizzes like every week?"

"Come, Watson," Benjamin said.

"Hey!" Mr. Hair yelled.

Nina and Benjamin stumbled past a surprised Marie and pelted down the stairs. But not quickly enough.

"Keith, what are you doing?" Lara cried.

What Keith was doing became apparent very quickly. He shoved past Nina on the landing and grabbed Benjamin by the neck. He pushed Benjamin rudely up against the wall. "You've been following me all damned night, pisshead."

"How could I be following you?" Benjamin said, sounding as reasonable as he could while being choked.

Nina launched herself at Keith, but he brushed her

169

aside with a sweep of his hand and she fell to her knees on the landing. Benjamin heard her cry out and swung with as much accuracy as he could—and at the close range, his accuracy was fairly good. His fist caught Keith on the side of his head. Keith released his hold, but there was no contest between a blind fighter and one who could see. Benjamin's follow-up swing caught air, and Keith sunk a fist into Benjamin's stomach, doubling him up.

Nina saw him fold and screamed, a sound that carried almost to the top of the stairs against the background noise of music and loud conversation.

Keith knelt over Benjamin and drew back his fist.

"No, you creep!" Nina yelled.

"Keith, don't!" Lara shouted.

Keith hesitated, fist still cocked. "He's been trailing us all night," he told her. "I have to teach this boy a lesson."

"Tell him to stop it," Nina said urgently to Lara.

Lara shrugged indifferently.

Benjamin took advantage of the momentary lull to lash out with his foot, which caught Keith in exactly the wrong place. At the same moment, Nina shouted, "Lara, he's your brother!"

Keith rolled back, clutching himself.

Benjamin struggled to his feet. He managed a swollen, misshapen smile, stuck his hand out in the general direction of Lara and said, "It's true, I am your half-brother, and I'd really appreciate it if you didn't let your boyfriend kill me."

Lara stared at him closely. Keith was up again, mostly recovered. "You're blind, aren't you?"

"Blind?" Keith grunted.

"Yep, I'm your blind half-brother Benjamin.

Later, if I'm still alive, I'll introduce you to your blond half-sister.''

The shoulders were unmistakable. It was Jake, Zoey was sure of that. And from the way he was swaying unsteadily as he tilted the bottle up, he had been drinking for a while.

She hesitated. Jake wasn't really her concern anymore. He was with Claire now. What she should do was go and find her, ask her to talk to him. But Jake was still her friend, wasn't he, even if he was no longer her *boyfriend*?

Zoey crossed the room. Lars spotted her coming and started giggling guiltily. Jake turned slowly, and his eyes met hers. She had expected cheerful, bleary drunkenness. What surprised her was the intensity of his gaze.

''Jake,'' she said gently. ''Why don't you come downstairs and dance with me?''

''Dance?'' His eyes might have been focused, but the rest of him was swaying six inches to either side. ''Can't, Zoey, sweet Zoey. I have to finish this bottle.'' He held up the half-empty bottle of tequila.

So much for indirect. ''Jake, you know you shouldn't be drinking,'' she said firmly.

He smiled wistfully. ''Do you care, Zoey?''

''Of course I care, Jake. You're my friend, and I don't like to see you hurting yourself this way.''

''Me?'' he asked softly. ''I'm not the one who's hurt, Zoey.''

From outside the room Zoey heard shouting, the sound of a scuffle or fight. The sight of Jake stinking drunk was profoundly depressing, and she wished she could just leave this party now. Benjamin and her half-sister, Jake hammered and hurting, some idiot fighting in the hallways. Where was Lucas, anyway?

Jake took another drink, defiant.

"Jake, stop it. You can't drink."

"Sure I can. Didn't you just see?"

Lars belched loudly and added, "He can definitely drink."

She grabbed Jake's arm and tried to pull him away, but even drunk, Jake was far too strong to be moved. She released him.

"Jake, I'm asking you as a friend who cares about you to stop this. You're just hurting yourself. I don't know if you had some kind of fight with Claire or what, but this isn't going to help."

"Yeah, I had a fight with Claire," he admitted. "She told me something interesting. You want to know what it was?"

"Probably not," Zoey said. She was losing patience. "It's personal between you two."

"Oh, no," he said, shaking his head emphatically. "It's not between just us."

A movement caught Lucas's eye. Yes, just what his instinct had told him—it was a fight. He had to squat a little to see what was happening on the stair landing. When he did, he was amazed to realize he was looking at Benjamin slipping to the ground with some guy standing over him, drawing back his fist.

Lucas muttered a curse and broke into a run. Halfway there, he saw Benjamin lash out with lucky accuracy, planting a foot in his tormentor's crotch. Lucas winced in automatic sympathy, then grinned in admiration. Benjamin had to know that the guy was just going to pound him twice as bad now. The boy was a piece of work.

He reached the steps and bounded up two at a time. There was a certain amount of loud talking, but to Lucas's surprise, the guy who had been pounding Benjamin now seemed to be just standing there, looking surprised. Standing there with legs together and a face that had a greenish tinge, but apparently not interested in carrying on the fight.

"Everything okay here?" Lucas asked.

Nina cocked an eyebrow at him. "If you're supposed to be the cavalry, you're late."

"Lucas, meet my half-sister, Lara," Benjamin said. "And her friend . . . Keith, right?"

"Keith," the guy said, gritting his teeth.

"Lucas Cabral," Lucas introduced himself. "I think I'll leave now." The situation looked under control, and like it involved private stuff that had nothing to do with him.

He'd find Zoey and ask her what this was all about. She'd taken off for the bathroom fifteen minutes ago, which, even for a girl, was a long time in the can. Especially since he'd seen Aisha return to the dance floor a few minutes ago.

He heard her voice and slowed down, trying to fix the direction. A door. He peeked around the corner. There was a couple making out on a bed. No, the guy had fallen asleep. In the corner Lars Ehrlich was sitting on the floor, hanging his head between his knees. Probably trying to keep from throwing up, Lucas decided.

Zoey was with Jake. Lucas bristled. She had a hand on his arm, trying to pull him away, but he resisted. "Hammered," Lucas said under his breath. "Plowed under."

He relaxed and hung back, just keeping them in sight. Jake didn't look much like a romantic threat right at the moment. In fact, it was obvious that Zoey was just trying to get him to stop drinking for a while. Lucas wondered whether Jake was an alcoholic. Could be. The guy didn't seem to know how to have *one* beer. When he drank, it was like slow-motion suicide.

Lucas had seen plenty of that type in the Youth Authority. Ninety percent of the guys in there were druggies or drunks or both. It was one of the reasons Lucas had so little interest in booze. Bunking with guys who would drink antifreeze to get drunk and then end up screaming about spiders on the way to the hospital in a straitjacket gave you a whole different perspective on alcoholism.

He stayed back from the doorway, out of sight, he hoped. No point in humiliating Jake any further by getting involved.

Zoey was talking to him, trying to be reasonable, a low murmur interrupted occasionally by some loud, slurred declamation from Jake.

It was impossible to be jealous. Zoey was just being Zoey, trying to make everyone feel better. Hard to be angry about that. Hard to feel bad about the fact that you were lucky enough to be going with a girl who was sweet and decent.

God, she was beautiful. God, he loved her.

"Oh, no," Jake said, shaking his head emphatically. "It's not between just us."

Lars had collapsed in the corner. "Jake, why don't we go outside and get some fresh air?" Zoey asked.

"Yeah. Yeah, that would be nice, Zo; you and me, just like the old days. You and me." He raised his head and looked at her. "You know what, Zoey?"

174

"What, Jake?"

"I still love you, Zoey. You know that? Not Claire, never Claire. Always you."

"Jake, you're just drunk and you're mad at Claire."

"No. I love you. Leave that guy, that Lucas, and come back to me, okay?"

There was a pathetic, puppyish look in his eyes. "Jake, I'm with Lucas now," she said.

He formed a half-smile. "And Lucas is with Claire."

"No, I think you're a little confused," Zoey said condescendingly.

"He screwed her," Jake said.

Zoey was about to dismiss the remark, but there was something in the way Jake had said it.

"They did it in the front seat of her daddy's Mercedes," Jake said.

"What are you talking about?"

"Lucas and Claire. Claire and Lucas. Sex. It. You know. She . . . she . . ." He was swaying dangerously now. "She said she liked it. That's what she said."

Zoey swung her hand palm open and slapped him across the face, a reflex action. He looked at her in shock. Slowly he reached up to touch the reddening patch on his cheek.

"It's true, Zoey," he said, sounding hurt.

Suddenly Zoey was aware of Lucas at her side.

"What's going on here?" he demanded, poised warily, as if he expected some sudden move from Jake.

"Too late, Cabral," Jake sneered. "I told her about you and Claire."

Zoey saw a look of pure horror on Lucas's face.

175

She felt as if all the blood had drained out of her in an instant. She took an unsteady step back.

"Zoey—" Lucas said, but had nothing else to offer.

"Get away from me," Zoey said.

"Zoey, no," Lucas pleaded.

"Get away from me!" Zoey screamed.

"Zoey, I love you!" Lucas cried.

Zoey ran.

Lucas reeled. He stared, horrified, at Jake. Jake wore a sickly look of triumph.

"What did you tell her?" Lucas demanded.

"I told her about you and Claire, you scumbag," Jake said.

Lucas flinched. Jake knew he had made out with Claire? "Who told you about that?" he demanded, knowing the answer.

"Who do you think?" Jake said.

"Look, it was just one of those things," Lucas said desperately. He was furious with Jake, but what could he say? He'd been making out with Jake's girlfriend behind his back. He wasn't exactly in a position to act all outraged. And then there was the fact that Jake was more than drunk enough to swing on him.

"Just one of those things?" Jake laughed. "I'll tell Claire you said that. You screw my girlfriend and it's just one of those things. Hear that, Lars, this little piece of crap sneaks around and screws *my* girlfriend and hey, it's no big deal." He had stopped swaying and was focusing dangerously now.

"Jake, what are you talking about, dude? I didn't screw Claire."

A malicious smile spread over Jake's face. A

smile with no hint of mirth. He slammed an open hand against Lucas's chest, shoving him back.

"Jake, I tried, all right?" Lucas said, holding up his hands placatingly. "We made out, I was mad at Zoey and Claire was there and one thing led to another."

Jake shoved him again, but with less conviction.

"Jake, that didn't happen. We didn't do it, man. Close but it never happened."

Behind the alcoholic haze, Jake's mind was working. "Claire said . . . Why would she . . . ?"

Lucas looked around in a wild parody of perplexity. "How in hell would I know why Claire does or says anything? But if she said we did it, she's lying."

Jake backed away a step. His brow wrinkled as he considered. Lucas was just as lost. Why would Claire lie like this? She had to have known if she told this story to Jake that Jake might tell Zoey. What motive did she have? Surely she hadn't just made up the lie without knowing where it would lead. Not Claire.

But that wasn't his problem right now. Right now his problem was what Zoey believed.

"Jake, I have to go, man. If you're going to pound on me, you have to do it now or let me walk. I'm not saying you don't have a right. It was low rent of me to be putting moves on Claire."

Jake nodded, but his real attention was far away.

"Sorry about this mess, Jake," Lucas said. "It was bad enough, but it wasn't what Claire said."

Again Jake nodded distractedly.

Lucas hesitated, torn between trying to settle this with Jake right now and the crying need to go after Zoey. He had to clear this up as fast as possible.

He'd tell Zoey the truth. That would be bad enough, but she could forgive him for that, couldn't she?

But if she believed what Jake had told her, she would never, ever forgive him. Not after what had been happening in her family.

He ran down the stairs, passing Nina and Benjamin, who were still talking to the couple who'd been trying to beat them up just minutes earlier.

Nina grabbed him as he went past. "What happened? Zoey just went tearing out the front door."

"Later, Nina," Lucas said. He ran outside and instantly realized he'd forgotten his coat. The temperature had dropped below freezing. He checked his watch. Five till nine. If Zoey was heading for the ferry, she'd be gone in five minutes. If he ran, he might still catch her. He might catch her, and she might believe him.

And if not . . . If he lost her . . .

No. He felt a thrill of fear, and the awful feeling that he had already lost the race. He ran as if his life depended on it.

Jake found Claire where he had left her. She seemed subdued, looking out of the high window at the street far below. He stood, waiting for her to notice him, still trying to collect his thoughts. The physical effects of the booze were still powerful. Standing straight was an effort, but parts of his mind were beginning to clear. He felt terribly weary. Too weary to try to be clever.

"Hello, Jake," Claire said placidly, still looking out of the window.

"It was a lie, wasn't it?" Jake said.

Claire said nothing.

"Why, Claire? What was the point?"

Claire's thin ghost of a smile appeared and evaporated. "Do you love me, Jake?"

Jake just stared. "What . . . what's that got to do . . ."

"Do you love Zoey?"

His eyes met hers. He looked away.

"And how do you think she feels about you, Jake?"

He shrugged. How *did* Zoey feel about him? Better than she felt about Lucas, now that she knew about him and Claire. Only he was forgetting—that hadn't really happened. That had just been a lie Claire told him.

Claire stood up. "Think it through, Jake," she sneered. "You just told her a lie about her boyfriend. You just told her Lucas slept with me. A lie. A pathetic lie you told because you wanted her back. Think it through, Jake," she snapped, suddenly furious.

"I don't . . . You're the one who told me," Jake protested.

"Me?" Claire looked surprised. "Why on earth would I go around telling people I slept with a guy I'm not even seeing? Why would I tell a lie like that?" She put her face close to his. Her beautiful, cold-eyed face. "Whereas you, Jake . . . You *would* make up a lie like that to get Zoey back. A low, contemptible trick to break up Zoey and Lucas, to take advantage of her vulnerability and get her to come back to you. How do you think Zoey will feel about you when she realizes you've done this to her, Jake?"

He looked at her in horror.

"You *and* Lucas," Claire said. "Both of you so

in love with Zoey. What was I, Jake? What was I?''

Her voice had lost its dangerous silkiness. It was ragged with emotion. He was stunned to see tears in her lustrous eyes. Despite everything, he couldn't help but feel some distant strain of pity mixed in with helpless despair at what she had done.

Her eyes blazed. ''Don't *you* feel sorry for me, you bastard.''

''I didn't know—I didn't think you cared.''

''Yeah, you're right,'' Claire said. ''I don't care. I don't have feelings. I don't have a heart, Jake. I'm just a cold, manipulative bitch. Well, that's what you thought, and tonight that's what you got. You hurt me, Jake. And when you hurt me, you damned well get hurt back.''

Lucas ran, through random, quick-melting snowflakes, down the cobblestoned streets, plowing through the groups of fashionable, yuppie-restaurant-crowd types, around the rowdy college-aged bar patrons.

The ferry's warning whistle sounded high and shrill. He ran full tilt, slipping on wet brick sidewalks, scrambling up, panting.

The ferry's whistle shrilled again. Too late, but he ran across the last street and slammed against the railing. The gangway was up and the ferry ropes cast off.

She was there, standing at the stern, looking down at him from her high perch.

''Zoey!'' he cried out, rattling the railing in his frustration.

Her face was set in rigid lines of bitterness.

''Zoey, it isn't true!'' he yelled. The ferry was

pulling away, a dozen feet of water already between them.

Slowly and deliberately, Zoey turned her back and disappeared.

Making Out:
Aisha Goes Wild

Cheating. Promises. Making up. What else could it be but book 8?

After **Zoey** breaks up with **Lucas,** and **Jake** breaks up with **Claire**, **Aisha** and **Christopher** are the only couple left on the island—until **Aisha's** old boyfriend Jeff comes back into her life. Everything changes on Halloween night when. . .

Aisha
Goes
Wild.

READ ONE...READ THEM ALL—
The Hot New Series about Falling in Love

MAKING OUT

by KATHERINE APPLEGATE